D0355824

Corbett fired instincti~~~~~~~~~~~~~~~ing, as he had taught himself to do throughout the years, and his bullet went true, catching the man in the back. He cried out, staggered and fell.

The outlaw beyond the horse, already moving forward, caught sight of Corbett and threw himself to his knees. He fired under the horse's neck, a quick snap shot that kicked up dirt inches from Corbett's face. Corbett found him then. He fired twice—once to get him in the legs to bring down his upper body, then a second time as the man fell . . .

Bantam Books by Frank Gruber
Ask your bookseller for the books you have missed

THE BIG LAND
THE CURLY WOLF
THE DAWN RIDERS

THE
CURLY WOLF
FRANK GRUBER

THE CURLY WOLF
A Bantam Book | July 1969
2nd printing .... February 1979

Cover art copyright © 1979 by Bantam Books

All rights reserved.
Copyright © 1969 by Frank Gruber.
This book may not be reproduced in whole or in part, by
mimeograph or any other means, without permission.
For information address: Bantam Books, Inc.

ISBN 0-553-06437-1

Published simultaneously in the United States and Canada

Bantam Books are published by Bantam Books, Inc. Its trade-
mark, consisting of the words "Bantam Books" and the por-
trayal of a bantam, is Registered in U.S. Patent and Trademark
Office and in other countries. Marca Registrada. Bantam
Books, Inc., 666 Fifth Avenue, New York, New York 10019.

PRINTED IN THE UNITED STATES OF AMERICA

Chapter One

Sam Forest was quite aware that he was commonly referred to as a curly wolf and did not object to the cognomen, even when it was used in the harshest range country connotation. He prided himself on the fact—and wanted people to know it —that he was at least ten degrees tougher than any man in the Seven Oaks Country.

Forest had been here first. He had sunk his spurs into this ground when the Holdermans were still in the mountains. He had already grazed considerable herds when Tom Hubbard made his appearance. He did not own the valley but he felt that it was his right to use as much of it as he felt necessary and the growth of his herds required him to use a great deal of it.

Forest had fought the Indians for this domain, he had fought the wild ones in the hills and he had fought the land itself and he had conquered all.

It was too late in the game for the Holdermans to steal from him and as for the Hubbard Ranch—yes, Tom Hubbard had been enough of a thief to do it, but Hubbard had been dead now for eight years and the Widow Hubbard—a widow would not challenge Sam Forest.

It had to be the Holdermans. Pete Holderman had come down from the hills sixteen or seventeen years ago, but he had never broken completely with the furtive ones who still lurked in the badlands.

Pete Holderman had three sons, but only two of them counted, Pete Jr., and Quincy, who were chopped from the same block as their sire.

The third son, Tracy, took after his mother. He had left the Holderman roost as soon as he was able to do so and was generally known as the *good* Holderman, to distinguish him from his brothers and father who by no stretch of the imagination could be fitted into the adjective "good"—or any of its synonyms.

The good Holderman had a few acres of his own, a tiny sliver of land that ran between a section of the Holderman and Forest ranches. He ran a few head of cattle and lived in a

1

structure that was little more than a shed, a one-room cabin that Tracy had built himself of logs and chinked with mud. He owned two horses and had never been seen to carry a gun of any kind.

He had as little as possible to do with his father and brothers, and if he ever visited their ranch it was not known.

On this last day of his life, Sam Forest had his usual hearty breakfast, although he was even more taciturn at the table than ordinarily. He did not talk at all to his wife and responded to his daughter's attempts at conversation with no more than a grunt or two.

He wiped a bit of egg from his chin and left the kitchen. Outside, he was starting toward the horse corral when he heard the pounding of galloping horses. He looked toward the left and saw two horsemen coming toward him. The riders were Barney McCorkle and one of the new hands that McCorkle had hired recently. He was an unshaven, shifty-eyed man. His clothing would have been disdained by a respectable scarecrow. But his revolver, that he wore low, was well-oiled and cared for.

Forest started toward the riders. They pounded up and McCorkle pulled his mount up to a violent stop. He dismounted lightly for so big a man and Forest wondered idly if his daughter would, finally, marry McCorkle. He hoped not.

The foreman of the Wolf Ranch nodded grimly. "About twenty-five, I'd say. Including that old mossy-back I put with the bunch, because he'd never stray off unless he was forced."

Forest nodded thoughtfully. "You followed their tracks?"

"Far enough to know they were headed for the rough country." McCorkle made an angry gesture. "How much longer are we gonna wait, Sam? They've already robbed us blind."

"I'm working on it," snapped Forest. "It ain't like the old days when you could stretch 'em where you caught 'em. You got to be damn sure you can prove it. Catchin' 'em with your stock ain't enough."

"Even if it's Pete Holderman?" asked McCorkle angrily.

"Pete's been hollerin' like a stuck pig," said Forest. "Claims he's lost twelve hundred head."

"That's a lot of hogwash and you know it."

"Maybe it is, but I want to be sure. A hundred and ten per cent sure."

"*I'm* sure," said McCorkle.

"Well, I'm not. But I'm going to be soon."

McCorkle's eyes narrowed. "You know somethin' I don't?"

Forest regarded his foreman thoughtfully and again wondered what his daughter saw in this man. An efficient fore-

2

man—Forest was willing to concede that, but he also wondered if there was not, somewhere, a "Wanted" poster on Barney McCorkle under another name.

McCorkle rode his horses too hard, he beat them too often and the ranch dog bared his teeth every time McCorkle came near to him.

An hour later, Sam Forest saddled his horse and mounted. His destination was the town of Seven Oaks, where he hoped there would be a letter for him from Chicago.

Forest jogged easily along the road toward Seven Oaks. He was aware of the horse grazing by the clump of cottonwoods but he did not see the man who was concealed there until he stepped out into the open.

The man had a double-barreled shotgun in his hands. He said, "Surprised, Sam?"

"No," replied Forest. "I been suspicionin' that it'd be you. I just wanted to be sure."

"Well, now you know," said the man with the shotgun. "You won't be needin' that detective you sent to Chicago for."

Forest went for his gun. His hand never reached it. The shotgun roared and Forest toppled from his horse. The killer came forward, pointed the shotgun down at Forest's head and pulled the second trigger.

Very little was left of Sam Forest's head.

The assassin broke the gun, took out the empty shells and put them in his pocket. He filled the barrels with fresh shells, snapped the gun shut and went to his horse. He mounted it and rode off at an easy gait. He did not look back.

Chapter Two

Six of the seven trees for which Seven Oaks had been named had been cut down and used for fuel during an unusually cold winter, but the seventh tree still stood near the county courthouse, where a low-hanging limb had once been used to hang a man after a mob had stormed the jail and taken out the victim.

Things were very quiet in Seven Oaks today. There were only two horses tied to the hitch rail in front of the Seven Oaks Saloon. Across the street, a single horse stood near the courthouse in the shade of the surviving oak tree.

Sheriff Link Brady, a heavy-set man, wearing his Sunday suit, came out of the courthouse and walked toward the horse nearby. He looked over his shoulder at the rider who was coming toward him. He saw a lean man wearing faded, patched Levis, a checked woolen shirt, a gun slung low on his right thigh, the holster tied down with a buckskin thong; another one of the kind that had been coming to Seven Oaks too often of late.

The stranger said to the sheriff, "Can you direct me to Sam Forest's ranch?"

The sheriff gestured up the street. "Straight ahead six miles." He hesitated. "Come for the funeral?"

The stranger's face showed no surprise, nor any other emotion. "Whose funeral?"

"Sam's," replied the sheriff. "We're buryin' him today."

"How did he die?"

The sheriff was aware that the stranger had asked *how*, not *when*. He said, "He was bushwhacked two days ago." Then, "You didn't come for the funeral?"

The man shook his head. "He wrote me a week ago, offering me a job."

"That figures." The sheriff climbed up on his horse. "You won't have any trouble getting another job. Pete Holderman will take you on, or the Widow Hubbard." The sheriff cleared his throat. "They're hiring guns."

He turned his horse and rode away.

Corbett looked after the sheriff a moment, then turned his

4

horse and rode to the hitch rail in front of the saloon. He dismounted, tied his horse to the rail and went into the saloon.

It was a long narrow place that could normally handle at least thirty patrons at the bar alone, but right now there were only two men at the mahogany.

They were an unkempt-looking pair who had apparently gotten an early start with their drinking. Corbett stopped at the bar a few feet from the other patrons.

"Beer," he said.

The bartender drew the beer and set the big glass before Corbett. He did not move away.

"Been riding a piece?" he asked.

"Too far," said Corbett. "Seeing as the job I expected has blown up." He quaffed deeply at his beer. "Man outside with tin on his vest told me they're planting the fella I come to work for."

One of the other patrons had heard Corbett. He grinned wickedly. "One thing I can't stand is a funeral."

His partner snickered. "Unless you caused it."

Corbett said, "You boys mourning for Sam Forest?"

The two men exchanged glances, then reaching an understanding, moved forward. The one who had spoken to Corbett hitched up his gun belt.

"Forest sent for you?"

Corbett nodded. "Said he had some work his people couldn't handle."

"Whoa-ho!" cried the first of the two early morning drinkers. "Looks like we got us a real rough one." He winked at his companion. "Mm, he's too old to be Billy the Kid, and John Wesley Hardin's in prison. Can't be him. Wyatt Earp, maybe?"

"Maybe Bat Masterson," said the second man.

"The name's Corbett," said Corbett. "Jim Corbett."

"Jim Corbett, huh?" The first man screwed up his face in concentration. "I guess I should know the name, but doggoned if I do. You heard it, Abe?"

"Uh-uh!" grunted the man called Abe.

"Well, let's see if he knows our names. Corbett, did you say? My paw called me Fess. For Festus. Fess Miller. My friend here answers to the name of Abe Hontz. Ever hear of us?"

"Can't say that I have," replied Corbett. "You boys been working for Sam Forest?"

The man who called himself Fess Miller spat copiously, not missing Corbett's feet by too much. "We was until yesterday when Forest's ramrod, McCorkle, fired us. Said the

5

widow don't intend to follow through on Sam Forest's schemes." He uttered a snort. "She don't know that ramrod! Wait until he marries the girl, Julie. He'll take over then and he'll be twice as rough as old Sam ever was."

"You ask me," said Abe Hontz darkly, "McCorkle wasn't too damn far away when Forest got bushwhacked."

"Abe," snapped Miller, "you're runnin' off at the mouth again."

"I ain't talkin' as much as you are," retorted Abe Hontz.

"Man as slow as you faces Barney McCorkle, it's like committin' suicide."

"McCorkle's fast with a gun?" asked Corbett.

"Plenty," said Miller. He hesitated. "The widow's brought in a couple of men are s'posed to be pretty good."

"Mrs. Forest?"

"Nah, the Widow Hubbard." Miller suddenly grunted. "Makes two widows now that're in it. The Widow Forest and the Widow Hubbard. Both tryin' to carve up Pete Holderman. Which'll take some doing."

"Who's likely to win?" asked Corbett.

Miller scowled. "If I knew that, I'd go to work for 'em. I was bettin' on Sam Forest, but I dunno if the ramrod can work behind the widow fast enough to make it go."

Corbett nodded thoughtfully. Then he fished a quarter out of his pocket and tossed it to the bar. The bartender picked it up, but made no move to bring any change. Beer was expensive in Seven Oaks.

Corbett headed for the door. Fess Miller called after him, "Who you gonna work for?"

"Myself," said Corbett, and went out of the saloon.

In his life, Sam Forest had had few, if any, friends. He had established an empire, which he had ruled with a hard fist and an ever-ready gun. As he grew older he had hired mercenaries to do his work for him and that had been good, but the trouble with having mercenaries is that your opponents can also hire them, and when you are playing that kind of game the rules are shucked aside.

Not that Peter Holderman had ever used any rules. He had been one of the predatory ones when Sam Forest had first made his bid for empire. There is a time for outlawry and there is a time when outlaws have to cease being outlaws. So Pete Holderman had come out of the badlands and established himself in Seven Oaks Valley. He brought with him three sons and a wife who did not live long. Holderman's herds prospered. He branded many calves, many mavericks.

6

He retained his contacts with the men in the mountains and it was very good for him in the big valley.

Sam Forest was a worthy opponent, as was Tom Hubbard. Holderman fought them and they fought him. Hubbard had finally died an ignominious death, thrown and stomped by a badly broken bronc.

And now Sam Forest was dead too. He had been cut down by a shotgun, but at least he had been facing his killer when death had struck him down and that was not too bad.

It was not much consolation to his widow and daughter, but surely they had known that a man who lives by a gun must sometimes die by one.

The funeral was a very fine one. People who had not set foot on the Wolf Ranch in ten years came for the final rites and tributes to the dead ruler of the ranch whose cattle brand was the head of a slavering wolf.

The Widow Hubbard attended the funeral bleak, unyielding, a fine figure of a woman if there had been a spark of compassion in her eyes.

Even the Holdermans had come: Old Pete and his sons Quincy and Pete Jr., and the good Holderman, Tracy, who had kept as far away as he could from his kin.

Corbett dismounted and tied his horse to the corral and, seeing the services already under way on the little knoll a hundred yards beyond the corral, he walked toward the large group.

The preacher was intoning the service in a vibrant voice that had already extolled the virtues of the departed one. He had dwelt at length upon Sam Forest's better qualities, magnifying them greatly, and had overlooked the traits that one usually forgets the moment the owner of them ceases to exist. Paraphrasing, in reverse, Shakespeare and Mark Antony:

> 'The good that men do lives after them,
> The bad is oft interred with their bones.'

The preacher was earning his fee, Corbett thought, as he stood at the edge of the—ah—mourners.

Corbett picked out the widow near the grave, a handsome woman of fifty, wearing black with a raised net veil. There were no tears in her eyes, nor were there any in the eyes of the younger woman beside her, her daughter Julie, who was possibly twenty-five, an extraordinarily attractive girl with dark blonde hair, clear-cut features, a taut face. She had loved her father, curly wolf that he was.

The preacher concluded his service and the pallbearers lowered the rough coffin into the grave. One of the pallbear-

7

ers, who instructed the others, was a strapping dark-haired man in his mid-thirties. He wore a black suit and a white tie. The suit seemed too small for him.

Corbett guessed that this man was the ramrod of the Wolf Ranch, Barney McCorkle. He became sure of his guess when the man moved to Julie's side after the coffin was well into the grave.

A few of the mourners filed past the grave; others moved away. Only one or two stopped to talk to the recently widowed Mrs. Forest and her daughter.

One of these was a woman in her early fifties, bleak, unyielding, but a fine-looking woman in spite of her tanned, rather weatherbeaten face with no spark of compassion in the eyes. She wore a dark blue dress, her graying hair piled high on her head. She turned away from the widow of Sam Forest and Corbett got a quick good look at her and knew who she was.

The Widow Hubbard.

She passed within twenty feet of Corbett, but her eyes looked straight ahead of her. Here and there a man or a woman spoke a greeting to her, but she gave only nodding response.

Corbett watched her go toward the corral, where she climbed into a buckboard to which was harnessed a team of excellent black geldings. She drove off, putting the horses into a good trot even before the buckboard reached the road. She drove left, toward the town of Seven Oaks.

Barney McCorkle was shaking hands with some of the departing men. Sheriff Link Brady spoke to him in a low tone and McCorkle's eyes sought out Corbett.

Corbett decided it was time to be leaving and started for the corral.

After a moment he heard footsteps behind him, coming up swiftly. Then a harsh voice snapped, "You—whatever your name is—wait!"

Corbett turned and waited for McCorkle to come up. There was a scowl on the big man's face.

"You told Link Brady that Forest sent for you," snapped McCorkle.

"That's right."

"What's your name?"

"Corbett."

McCorkle shook his head. "Sam never sent for anyone name of Corbett."

"You're calling me a liar?"

"I will—if it's necessary. Sam never hired anyone without

8

talking it over with me." McCorkle held out his hand. "Let me see the letter."

Corbett regarded the foreman thoughtfully. "If I still had the letter I wouldn't show it to you."

McCorkle's face distorted in anger. "This is no time for a showdown, but if you'll wait in Seven Oaks until tomorrow I'll find you and then I'll call you a liar to your face."

Corbett turned his back on the foreman and walked off. He reached his horse and was mounting when a short, stocky man of about thirty came hurrying up to him. "Pa wants to talk to you," the man said.

Corbett looked at him inquiringly. "I'm Quincy Holderman," the man said. "Paw saw you fussin' with McCorkle and says to tell you to come out to the ranch." Quincy looked over his shoulder. "He don't want to be seen here talkin' to you."

Corbett nodded thoughtfully. "I'm not sure I want to be seen talking to him, so tell your pa I'll be at the hotel in Seven Oaks for a few days. He can come there."

"He wants you to come out to the ranch."

"I'll be at the hotel," said Corbett, and rode off.

Chapter Three

The Seven Oaks Hotel was a two-story building with lobby and dining room on the first floor and ten very small rooms on the second floor. Corbett drew Room 5, which was six-by-eight feet in size and contained a cot, a straight-backed chair and a washstand, on which were a pitcher and a cracked washbowl. Some nails had been driven into the wall, and were obviously intended to take the place of a clothes closet.

Corbett unrolled his bedroll and found several sheets of paper and envelopes. He removed the washbowl and pitcher from the stand and, seating himself before it, wrote a letter addressed to *Peter Drucker, Box 14-A, Chicago, Illinois.*

The letter was short. It read:

Dear Peter:

Regret to inform you that Sam Forest was bushwhacked two days ago by a person unknown. I have just attended his funeral and will remain here in Seven Oaks until I hear from you. I suggest you reply by telegraph, merely saying yes if you wish me to investigate, and no if you want me to drop the matter.

Yours truly,
James Corbett.

He addressed the envelope and, inserting the letter, sealed it. Then he left his room and descended to the hotel lobby, where Milo Gregson, the proprietor of the hotel, was now presiding.

"Can you tell me if there is a post office in town?" Corbett asked him.

Gregson held out his hand. "Got a letter? I'll mail it for you."

"I'll mail it myself," said Corbett.

Gregson shrugged. "Brady's Store."

"Brady? The sheriff . . . ?"

"His brother Jeff." Gregson waited until Corbett had

reached the door, then added, "Don't waste time with the girl."

Corbett looked at him sharply. Gregson grinned. "She's spoken for. Tracy Holderman, the *good* Holderman."

"There's a good Holderman as well as one not good?"

The hotel man whistled. "Old Pete's as ornery as a Longhorn bull with a cactus spike under his tail. His older boys, Quincy and Pete Junior, are practicin' to outdo the old man, but Tracy, well, he left the nest early and wants no part of the family."

"It's still the same blood."

Gregson shrugged. "I wouldn't say it to Pete's face, but I dunno, Tracy's as different from the rest of his family as—well, as day is from night."

Corbett nodded thoughtfully and left the hotel. He had no difficulty finding Brady's store. It was just beyond the Seven Oaks Saloon and was about forty feet wide and with a depth of perhaps sixty feet.

The store was an emporium that must have been a great delight to all the ranchers' wives and children. It contained everything from clothing to guns, barbed wire to sugar, potatoes to percale.

A man a few years older than the sheriff, but with a strong family resemblance, was behind the long counter that ran down the left side of the store. He nodded to Corbett.

Corbett held up the letter and continued to the rear of the store where a sign over a wicket said POST OFFICE. A very attractive young lady, wearing a black muslin apron over a checked dress, was behind the wicket.

"I'd like to get a stamp for this letter," Corbett said.

"We got a special on stamps this week," said the girl brightly. "Twenty-five cents' worth for a quarter."

"I guess I can't refuse a bargain like that," said Corbett. He put a quarter on the counter. "Tell me, how long will it take for this letter to reach Chicago?"

The girl pursed up her lips. "Well now let's see, the stage should be along in an hour or two, unless it's broken a wheel again. But saying it's on time, which it never is, this here letter will be in Roswell around midnight—that is, if the driver doesn't get drunk on the number 8 relay station. But if it *does* get to Roswell tonight, it'll be in Tucumcari sometime tomorrow and if it gets on the train tomorrow it ought to be in Chicago in four or five days. That is, if it don't get on the westbound train by mistake. But with luck, the letter should be in Chicago in about a week."

"A week!" exclaimed Corbett. "Before I know whether I stay or leave your great city. What can a man do for a week

—since the most beautiful girl here is already spoken for."

"Who's spoken for?"

"You."

"And who told you a whopper like that?"

"It isn't true?"

"If it is, I haven't been told—yet."

Corbett grinned. "Well now, I don't want to start a war, but when I asked the way to the post office a man told me not to waste my time on you—'cause you were already spoken for."

"Did this—this person who knows more about me than I know myself, tell you who it was who's spoken for me?"

"He said it was the *good* Holderman. Who was not to be confused with the bad Holdermans."

"Mister," said the girl behind the wicket, "you've got a name?"

"James Corbett. It's on the back of the letter."

"I saw the name on the letter—but I'd rather get a person's name from the person hisself. Especially when he's a man like yourself."

"Well, I've gone this far, I may as well see it through. What's a man like myself?"

"You're not a drummer," said the girl, "because you're not dressed well enough. That means also that you're not a gambler, because they dress even fancier than the drummers. You look like a cowboy, but—" she held up a detaining hand. "Don't tell me now, let me guess—mmm, yes, you *could* be an outlaw . . ."

"No," said Corbett.

"You're not a cowboy, you're not an outlaw . . ."

"I didn't say I wasn't a cowboy; *you* said that."

"I said it, and I'll stick by it." She suddenly snapped her fingers. "You're a gun fighter!"

"Wrong again."

"I give up. What *do* you do?"

"Nothing—right now. I'm unemployed."

She shook her head. "The sheriff's my uncle. He doesn't like unemployed people hanging around town. He calls 'em bums. Are you—a bum?"

Corbett chuckled. "I've never thought of myself as one. I had one job for fifteen years."

She brightened. "What kind of work was that?"

"Well, I wore a uniform. A blue uniform with broad yellow stripes down the trousers."

"A cavalryman. Fifteen years? Mmm, no, I guess even Uncle Link couldn't call you a bum, even though you're out of work now."

"Does that qualify me?"

"For what?"

"For taking you to dinner, or—well, what *do* people do in Seven Oaks?"

"Well, there's a dance at the Town Hall about once every month but there was one only last week, so it's going to be a while before there's another."

"The dinner, then?"

She hesitated. "Ask me tomorrow and if I'm not spoken for by then . . ."

He winced. "You're seeing the good Holderman tonight?"

"I'm seeing him now—right behind you . . ."

Corbett had been so engrossed in the chitchat with the girl that he had not heard anyone coming into the store, but he wheeled now and saw a stocky man in his late twenties standing by the counter talking to Jeff Brady, the proprietor.

His eyes met Corbett's. It was obvious to Corbett that he had heard the description of himself, but was going to pretend that he had not.

Corbett gave the girl a last look, drew a deep breath and went toward Tracy Holderman.

"I'm Jim Corbett," he said. "I believe I saw you at the funeral."

Tracy Holderman nodded shortly. "You're the man came to work for Forest."

"Oh-oh, that's gotten around," said Corbett.

"Barney McCorkle's a friend of mine," said Holderman.

"But not of your brothers?"

"Mister," said Tracy Holderman deliberately, "you're a stranger here, so I won't take offense, but my name *is* Holderman and I don't take kindly to derogatory remarks about *anyone* named Holderman."

"Well," said Corbett, "that's a fair statement. I'll keep it in mind." He nodded, sent a quick look back toward Cathy Brady, then left the store.

He walked toward the hotel, where his horse was hitched to the rail. Gregson, the hotel proprietor, came out.

"Get your letter mailed?"

"Yes—and it isn't true what you said, that the girl's spoken for."

"Then Tracy Holderman's a lot stupider than I figured him for. He's been makin' sheep's eyes at Cathy for more than a year. What's he waitin' for?"

"Competition, maybe."

Gregson regarded Corbett thoughtfully. "You aim to stay in Seven Oaks awhile?"

"Perhaps." Corbett made a small gesture. "You've heard,

of course, that Sam Forest sent for me and I'm sure you've also heard that the widow isn't doing any more hiring. So—can you direct me to the ranch of the other widow, the Widow Hubbard?"

"She sets a good table, I hear," said Gregson, "but she don't pay as well as Sam Forest used to. On the other hand, the Holdermans don't pay regular wages at all. Just a share of what you can steal for them."

"That's really laying it on the line," said Corbett.

Gregson shrugged. "This business has been going on a long time. There's not much secrecy about any of it."

"Except who bushwhacked old Sam, eh?" Corbett watched Gregson carefully. "Who's your candidate for that?"

"That's a horse of another color."

"Is it?"

Gregson drew a deep breath, exhaled, then suddenly turned and went into the hotel.

Chapter Four

Corbett saw the cluster of buildings that was headquarters for the Hubbard Ranch even before he turned off the main road onto the road that led from it to the ranch. The buildings were dominated by a white, two-story frame house that had pillars running along the front of it; a house that would have been more appropriate to an eastern state than New Mexico.

Not far from the big house was a smaller one, built of adobe bricks, a one-story building that contained perhaps two or three rooms and which had been the original home of the Hubbards when they had first settled here. It was now used by the foreman of the ranch.

Some fifty yards from the foreman's house were two one-story frame houses, bunkhouses, and beyond them were barns, outhouses and corrals.

It was a substantial layout, indicating a large and prosperous ranch.

As Corbett sat his horse, surveying the domain, the ruler of it came from the nearest corral, passing between the bunkhouses.

Corbett watched her approach, a vigorous, proud woman. A strong woman.

She was aware of his presence, but did not come directly toward him. She would have passed him by thirty feet in her passage, but suddenly she wheeled and came toward him. She stopped ten feet away and looked up at him, taking in every detail of him.

Corbett regarded her as fully as she did him. He nodded slightly.

"Ma'am."

She said evenly, "It's twenty years, isn't it?"

"Just about."

Alice Hubbard exhaled heavily. "I thought about this many times and I had the words memorized, but now that the time's come, I can't seem to remember what they were."

"I made up a little speech myself," said Corbett, "but I can't seem to remember it either."

"I shed my last tears in '59," Alice Hubbard said evenly.

"Tears, ma'am?"

"Ma'am," she repeated. "Is that the way you've thought about me all these years?"

Corbett made no reply and she went on heavily, "Tom Hubbard died eight years ago. When I buried him, I buried all the things I remembered about him, the good and the bad."

"He was very good," said Corbett, "with the handle of a pitchfork."

"Is that why you've come here?" asked Alice Hubbard. "To tell me how you were mistreated when you were a boy?"

"No, ma'am," said Corbett easily. "The reason I came to Seven Oaks is that Sam Forest sent for me."

Her eyes went to the Winchester in the scabbard, to the revolver along his thigh. A heaviness seemed to come over her and she said flatly, "So that's what you've become!"

"The first man I talked to when I got here this morning was the sheriff. He told me about Sam and said that I'd have no trouble getting work. He said the Holdermans were hiring guns—and the Widow Hubbard."

Her eyes blazed for one brief instant, then she lidded them. But she did not speak.

"Ma'am," went on Corbett, "I'm very good at my work. I killed my first man before I was even seventeen and I guess if I did that sort of thing, I could cut maybe thirty-forty notches in my gun—and that's not even counting Indians."

"When you get through," said Alice Hubbard, "I'll get back to my work."

Corbett drew a deep breath and exhaled. He held up his hand in a small salute. "Ma'am."

He turned his horse and rode away at an easy lope.

Alice Hubbard went into the house. She seated herself in a wooden rocking chair and rocked it gently back and forth.

In a ranch house some eight miles from the Hubbard house, another widow sat in a rocking chair, her mind crowded with memories. But she was not alone. Her daughter Julie was in the room with her. The younger woman had set the kitchen table at two o'clock, had put out the food, but her mother had eaten none of it. Julie had cleared off the table, washed the dishes. She worked about the kitchen as long as she could restrain herself.

"Why don't you sell the ranch?" she finally burst out.

Her mother did not reply but after awhile stopped rocking her chair. Julie, going around in front of her, saw that her mother had come to some decision.

16

"No," Mrs. Forest said finally. "Your father's buried here and this is where I stay—until you bury me too."

"But you never liked the ranch," protested Julie Forest. "You told Dad over and over that you wanted to give it up. You told me . . ."

"I don't like the ranch," said Mrs. Forest, "I don't like the things that have been done—that must be done—but your father didn't like them either."

"He loved the ranch!" cried Julie Forest. "It was his whole life."

"That was what he wanted people to think," said Mrs. Forest. "I—I know. He didn't talk about it, not in years. He just did—what had to be done. But years ago, when we first came here, he—he would turn to me at night. Sometimes he would actually be ill from—from something that happened during the day, something that he'd had to do. A fight, perhaps—" she stopped. "He'd had too much of it, he was old. I guess that's why he sent for the detective."

"Detective?" cried Julie.

"I haven't opened the mail in the last couple of days," said Mrs. Forest. "I found this about an hour ago . . ."

She drew a folded letter from the pocket of her dress and handed it to Julie.

Julie opened the letter, began reading aloud:

. . . The terms you outlined in your letter are satisfactory and I have today dispatched a detective to your community. He is one of our very best operators and I have always found him exceedingly discreet. He will remain incognito and will reveal his identity only to you. He is a man of considerable experience, both as a detective and in his previous capacity, which I need not detail here. Suffice to say, I trust him implicitly and consider him especially qualified in handling a dangerous assignment as you say yours may turn out to be. Thanking you for the check, I remain,

> Yours very truly,
> Amos Jarvis
> Jarvis Detective Agency.

Julie looked up from the letter and stared at her mother. "Didn't—didn't Dad tell you he was sending for the detective?"

Mrs. Forest shook her head. "I am sure he did not want to worry me. It's one of the very few things he ever kept from me."

"This detective, the letter doesn't say when he's due to arrive."

17

"It says that he was being dispatched the same day as the letter. It's dated five days ago. He could have reached here by now."

"Yes," said Julie suddenly. "There was a stranger at the funeral today. Barney told me about him afterwards. He said the man claimed to have been sent for by Dad, but as a—a gunhand. Barney was miffed that Father hadn't told him about the man."

"Then it was because he didn't want Barney to know." Mrs. Forest frowned. "That was one thing your father did say to me just the day before—" she shook her head, drew a deep breath, then went on firmly, "He said he had gotten to the point where he couldn't trust anyone."

"But Barney's our foreman. He's been with us for four years. Besides—" Julie stopped. "Did Dad ever tell you what he thought about—about Barney and me?"

There was a shade of hesitance before Julie's mother replied. "He always said that you had to live your own life, that we had no right to criticize or interfere with your choice of a husband."

"Mother," said Julie, "I want the truth. You *must* tell me. Father didn't actually like Barney, did he?"

"Your father's dead, Julie. I am not going to break faith with him, not now."

Julie was silent for a long moment, then she came to a decision. "Have you decided what to do about the—the detective?"

"I've just been thinking about it, Julie. I—I frankly don't know what to do. Apparently your father sent a check to the agency in Chicago. All we can do, I guess, is let them keep the money and tell the man to go back to Chicago. I'm not certain that it's the right thing to do, but I don't know what else."

"Mother," said Julie slowly, "you know even better than I that if there was one thing Dad hated, it was a quitter. Once he started something he always finished it. Isn't that so?"

Her mother nodded. "You think that we should have the detective go ahead and do what he was hired to do?"

"Yes, I know it's the right thing. I know Dad would want it."

"I'm inclined to agree with you. In fact I had almost come to that decision myself. Talking it over has made me see that it is what your father would have wanted." She exhaled heavily, in relief. "I'll tell the detective then to go ahead when he arrives."

"Why wait, Mother? If the stranger who was out here today is actually the detective, there's only one place he could

18

be. At the hotel in Seven Oaks. I'll go into town, tell him what you've decided . . ."

Julie hurried into her room, changing her clothes to Levis, a wool shirt and boots. She left the house within a few minutes and strode swiftly to the corral. She took down a lasso from a post, went into the corral and caught her horse. She led him out of the corral and began to saddle him.

She was tightening the cinch when Barney McCorkle came up. "Where are you going?" he asked.

"For a ride. I've got tired of staying in the house."

"Wait until I catch my horse," said McCorkle. "I'll ride with you."

"No," said Julie quickly. "I want to be alone."

"That's all right," said McCorkle easily. "I'll just tag along. I'll just be there in case you change your mind and want to talk."

"I'm going to town," said Julie irritably, "and I want to go alone."

"All right, all right," said Barney. "I know you're nervous and upset by what's happened, but you don't have to snap my head off."

"I didn't mean to snap at you, Barney. It's just—well, what you said. I *am* nervous and I thought I'd go into town. I'm not going to stay there very long."

Barney McCorkle nodded and caught her arm. He attempted to turn her so that he could embrace her, but she pushed him away. "I'm not in the mood, Barney!"

His temper, always smoldering, flared up. "The hell with that, Julie! There've been too damn many times lately that you haven't been in the mood and I'm gettin' pretty fed up with it. You and your mother need me to run this ranch . . ."

"I think you've said about enough, Barney," cried Julie, becoming coldly angry.

"I haven't said half of what I'm going to say. You're in the middle of a range war, a war that your pa was as much responsible for as anyone. Which reminds me, I haven't forgotten that he sent for a man without talkin' to me about it. After all the things I've done for him . . ."

"He didn't trust you, Barney," snapped Julie. "He didn't tell you about the detective because he didn't trust you."

"Detective?" cried McCorkle. A swift change sobered him. "That gunslick's a detective?"

Julie realized that she had let it slip and tried to cover up. "I don't know. I—I saw him today when he was out here. And he could be a detective. But I don't really know. At any rate, it's too late—for a detective . . ."

19

"Damn it," swore McCorkle. "Of course he's a detective! I should have known—" a sudden gleam came into his eyes. "Well, I'll soon send him packing."

He headed for the corral gate. "Barney," cried Julie in panic. "What are you going to do?"

"I'm going into town and tell him that the Forest family doesn't need a detective and to get the hell out of Seven Oaks."

"No, you mustn't," said Julie. "Mother and I've talked it over. We *do* want the detective to stay here . . ."

But McCorkle was not listening. He stormed into the corral and headed for his favorite saddle mount.

Julie stood beside her saddled horse a moment, shocked by the sudden turn of events. Then she came to a quick decision, sprang into the saddle and, turning the horse, started it off at a full run.

Chapter Five

The hotel dining room was known far and wide in Seven Oaks for its excellent menu, which consisted of two entrees, beefsteak and beef stew. Corbett chose the steak, which was served with soggy, boiled potatoes. Dessert consisted of canned peaches. Corbett had eaten many worse meals in his time and when he finished he paid his dollar cheerfully. He bought a cigar at the hotel desk and, seating himself on a bench outside the hotel, lit the cigar and watched the street come to life. Later, he thought, he would have a beer or two and perhaps play cards for awhile.

He had half-finished his cigar when he became aware of the pounding of horses' hoofs. A rider was coming pell-mell up the street. The rider wore boots, Levis and a man's shirt but was definitely a woman. The destination was the hotel and as the rider dismounted, Corbett saw that it was Julie Forest. She threw the reins over the hitch rail and came toward Corbett.

"You're the detective," she said flatly.

Corbett could not restrain a wince and exclamation. He started to get to his feet. "I've been called a lot of things in my time—" he began.

The girl cut him off with an impatient gesture. "I haven't got time to waste. You were at the funeral this morning and you're the only stranger in town. *Are* you, or are you not the man my father sent for?"

Corbett sent a quick look around. There was no one within earshot on the street, but the hotel proprietor was at his desk inside and if he strained his ears he could hear the dialogue outside.

He said in a low tone, "Yes, your father sent for me."

"Barney McCorkle says you're a gun fighter," cried Julie Forest. "I've got to know for sure. *Are* you a gun fighter? Or a detective?"

"Miss," said Corbett awkwardly, "your father's dead. Whatever reason he sent for me no longer exists."

"I asked you," she said fiercely, *"are you a detective?"*

Corbett drew a deep breath and let it out heavily. "Yes."

"Why did my father send for you?"

"All I know is the letter he sent to my employer—with a check. He said somebody was trying to kill him and he wanted a man to come down and arrest the person."

"Did he say who it was?"

"No. Apparently he didn't know. Although he didn't say that exactly. He did mention that there was a range war going on between him and a couple of ranchers and things had gotten to the point where he couldn't trust anyone."

"You said my father sent a check. How much?"

"Five hundred dollars. He said he would pay another thousand when the job was finished."

"Do it," said Julie Forest. "Find the man who killed my father!"

Corbett hesitated. "Wouldn't that be up to your mother to say?"

"I didn't come here on my own," said Julie. "I talked it over with mother first. She—she wants you to get the man who killed Dad."

Corbett looked past Julie to a horse that was coming toward them at an easy canter. It was ridden by Barney McCorkle.

"What about your foreman?" said Corbett easily. "Barney McCorkle."

"He's got nothing to say about this," snapped Julie. "He isn't a member of the family—yet." Then she heard the horse coming up behind her and turned.

McCorkle's eyes were slitted; his jaw muscles twitched. He swung down from his horse, ignored Julie and moved toward Corbett.

"Mr. Detective," he said, "you've got a half hour to get the hell out of town."

"Barney," cried Julie, "you had no right to follow me."

"Somebody's got to look after you," declared McCorkle, "and who's got a better right than me?"

"You're a hired hand," said Julie Forest cuttingly. "You can be fired."

McCorkle did not like that at all but instead of retorting to Julie, he turned back to Corbett. "Start moving . . ."

His right hand went out involuntarily to push against Corbett to enforce his command. It never touched Corbett, for Corbett's fist came up and cracked against McCorkle's jaw. It was a hard blow and McCorkle reeled to one side. He caught himself and, crouching, stared at Corbett in utter astonishment.

"I'm glad you did that," he gasped. "Saves argument." He

started forward. "I'm gonna thrash you within a half-inch of your life. That'll teach you."

He sprang forward suddenly, flailing away with both hands.

Corbett was prepared. He stepped to one side, caught the edge of one of the blows on his shoulder, then hit McCorkle in the stomach with every ounce of his weight behind the blow.

McCorkle bent forward gasping. His hands crossed over his stomach and he fell to his knees, then to his face. He thrashed for a moment, then sucking in air, managed to get back to his knees. Still clawing at his stomach, he looked up at Corbett.

"I could kick you in the face," said Corbett coldly, "which is probably what you'd do in my case, but I'll wait for you to get up."

McCorkle struggled to his feet and Corbett took a step forward, but McCorkle, still holding his stomach, staggered to one side. He went to his horse, mounted with difficulty, but then turned it toward Corbett.

"You're a dead man, detective," he said, then turned his horse and rode away.

"That," said Gregson the hotel man standing behind Corbett, "is the first time Barney McCorkle's been licked—and it couldn't happen to a nicer fellow."

Julie Forest's face was a study in misery. She looked from Corbett to the retreating McCorkle, then back to Corbett.

"You—you'll do what I asked you to?" she asked waveringly.

Corbett nodded. "Yes."

She whirled then, ran to her horse and piled up into the saddle. She started the animal off at a full gallop after Barney McCorkle.

Corbett watched her. Gregson moved up beside him. "So you're a detective, hey?"

Corbett gave him an angry look. "Damn it, keep it to yourself. Too many people know it already."

The hotel man chuckled wickedly. "All we needed in Seven Oaks was a detective—" He stepped quickly away from Corbett and held up a detaining forefinger. "I'm on your side, Corbett. I never did like Barney McCorkle, and any man who can lick him can't be all bad."

Corbett started away from Gregson in the direction of the saloon, but before he had gone more than twenty steps a man crossing the street intercepted him. He was a rather short, stocky man in his early thirties. He wore broadcloth trousers

23

and a coat, but nickle gleamed from a badge pinned to his vest.

He said to Corbett, "What was that ruckus with McCorkle?"

Corbett stopped. "He didn't like my face and tried to change it."

The man nodded. "Your life insurance paid up?"

"I haven't got any."

"I'd get some, I was you." The man made a small gesture. "My name's Smith. I work for the sheriff. Eben Smith, just so you know."

"Eben Smith," repeated Corbett thoughtfully. "I've heard of you but from what I heard I didn't think you'd be wearing a badge."

"Link says Sam Forest sent for you. You figure on stayin' here awhile?"

"Awhile."

Eben Smith nodded. "Link says he couldn't care less what you fellows do to each other." Then a sharpness came into his voice. "But keep it among yourselves or you'll be facing me."

"And that wouldn't be good, eh?"

"I took this job because I got tired of people trying to gun me down and I didn't like the runnin' all the time. But I didn't get any slower, if you know what I mean." Smith made an expressive gesture. "I get sixty dollars a month and I pick up a little reward money once in awhile." He paused and regarded Corbett thoughtfully. "Are there any reward posters out on you?"

"No."

"We get them in all the time. I'll find out if there are."

"I'm not wanted—anywhere."

Smith nodded thoughtfully and went off. Corbett continued on to the saloon.

He found the place already well patronized, with seven or eight imbibers at the bar and two poker games going on at tables.

Corbett ordered a beer and as he sipped it he sized up the poker games. One table had five players, the other only four. One of the players at the table of five was Jeff Brady, the brother of Link Brady the sheriff.

Corbett finished his beer and strolled over to the more populated table.

"Is this a private game," he asked, "or can anyone lose money in it?"

One of the players gestured to the nearby table. "They need an extra player."

24

Corbett looked pointedly at the money before the players. "There's more money in this game."

Brady indicated a chair. "Pull up a chair."

Corbett went around to the indicated chair and sat down. He took out a sheaf of bills. "What're you playing?"

"Draw poker," replied Brady. "Five dollars limit."

"Five dollars per card?"

"Five per bet," said Brady.

"And no limit to the number of bets? Sounds like a good game."

"It's been lousy," snapped one of the players.

Corbett looked at the remaining few bills before the man and chuckled. "By the way, my name's Jim Corbett."

Brady nodded. "We know all about you. Small town. I'm Jeff Brady." He indicated the man at his right. "Tolliver." He nodded to the next man. "Blake. Menzies and our Wells Fargo agent, Dick Bonner . . ."

The last named man, who had the least amount of money before him, scowled. "Who won't be in the game if he loses two more hands!"

"Dollar ante," said Menzies, who was dealing.

Corbett put a dollar into the pot. Menzies dealt swiftly. Corbett put his cards together tightly and, squeezing them, examined the luck of the deal. He found a pair of kings, an ace, a seven and a four.

The man on his right, who was first, said, "Pass."

Corbett looked at the dealer. "What does it take to open?"

"Jacks."

Corbett nodded. "I pass."

Bonner scowled. "Stuck again. I open for a dollar."

Brady, who was next, tossed in a silver dollar. "If it gets higher, I quit."

The next man threw in his hand, which brought it to the dealer. "We'll get rid of the pikers," he said. "Up five." The man on Corbett's right promptly threw his cards into the discard.

Corbett hesitated. "I just want to see how you boys play poker." He put in six dollars.

Bonner snarled, "Goddam jacks get me into trouble every time." However, he put in five dollars. Brady followed, without comment.

"Cards?" asked the dealer.

"Two," said Corbett. Then he smiled feebly. "Kicker."

The Wells Fargo man snorted, "One of those! Three for me."

"One," said Brady.

"Straight or flush," murmured the dealer. He dealt himself one card, but did not look at it. "Dealer takes one."

Corbett mixed his draw cards with the three he had held and again squeezed them carefully. He had drawn a third king and now had three kings, the ace kicker and a jack.

"I'll see where the strength is," he announced. "Check."

Bonner scowled heavily. "I'm in this far. I might as well go whole hog. Five." He put out a bill, which left him with less than ten dollars.

"Call," said Brady quietly.

The dealer still did not look at his draw card. "All right, I'll bet blind—and hope. Five and five."

Bonner swore roundly. "Ten up to me," said Corbett. He counted out the money, threw in an extra five dollars. "And five."

"You and your kicker," snarled Bonner. He counted out his money. "I'm a dollar short."

Brady said, "You know it's table stakes. You calling for just the nine?"

"What else?"

Brady shrugged. "Because I'm raising it five."

"Whoa!" cried the dealer. He caught up his new card, looked at it and searched Brady's face. "You bluffing, Jeff?"

"Raise me and find out."

The dealer waited a long moment, then tossed in his cards. Corbett said, "I'll raise it five."

The Wells Fargo man cried out, "You connected with your kicker?"

Corbett shrugged.

"I got the best hand," complained Bonner bitterly, "and I can't bet it."

"You can as far as I'm concerned," said Corbett. "Nobody told me at the beginning that it was table stakes."

The Wells Fargo man pounced on it. "How about it, Brady?"

Brady hesitated. "The stranger's got a point, but . . ."

"Just this once!" cried Bonner. "I've been losing all evening."

"It's all right with me," said Corbett.

"In other words," said Brady to Bonner, "you caught a good one."

"I haven't heard much from you," accused Bonner. He turned to Corbett. "Okay with you?"

Corbett nodded. Brady exhaled. "All right, all right."

"I owe eleven in the pot," said Bonner quickly, "and I raise it five."

26

"I knew it!" cried Brady. "You caught a third to your openers!"

"Pay and find out."

Brady looked at his cards, shook his head, then suddenly looked across at Corbett. "I call," he said and put out another ten dollars.

"I call the raise and add five more," said Corbett.

Bonner's startled eyes tried to peer behind Corbett's slitted ones. "Wa-ait, you asked what it took to open. Then you said kicker. That'd indicate a small pair and a kicker. You mighta got another pair, or—you drew a third to your pair."

"No law says a man's got to tell the truth," said Corbett.

"You're bluffing," cried Bonner, "or you got aces up to your kicker!" He hesitated. "I call and . . ."

He scowled.

"Yes?" asked Corbett.

Bonner collapsed. "I'll just call."

"Just to keep it honest," said Brady. He put in five dollars and spread out his hand. "Queens and treys."

"Three jacks," cried Bonner, unable to wait for Corbett.

"Kings," said Corbett. "Three of them."

A stricken look came over Bonner. "I walked into that. No wonder you let me owe . . ."

"I thought he had us all the time," said Brady cheerfully.

"I owe you sixteen dollars," said Bonner.

"Twenty-one," corrected Corbett. "You called my raise."

"That's right, twenty-one." Bonner pushed back his chair. "I—I'll pay you in the morning."

He got up from his chair. Eben Smith moved up, sat down easily. "Poker pays better than detecting," he observed. A sudden silence fell upon the immediate group. Smith, seeing all eyes fixed on Corbett, chuckled wickedly. "Deal me in. Always wanted to see if a detective could play poker." Then he assumed a bland look of innocence and looked around the group. "I spill something, boys? What'd you think he was? A drygoods drummer?"

Corbett finished straightening out his winnings. He suddenly folded the bills. "Guess I'll get to bed early tonight." He pushed back his chair preparatory to getting up.

"Don't go," said Smith, throwing out a detaining hand. "I'm new at this law business and I'd kinda like to watch you operate. Maybe I can pick up some pointers. What's the outfit you work for? Pinkerton? No—uh, oh yes, The Jarvis Agency in Chicago. I've heard tell they're awfully good."

Corbett stuffed his money into a pocket and got to his feet. "Good night, gentlemen."

"You always quit when you're winning?" challenged Eben Smith.

"That's the best way," said Corbett. He nodded and turned away.

Smith sent one more taunt after him. "You gonna make your daily report to Jarvis?"

As Corbett neared the Seven Oaks Hotel he saw that a man was seated on the bench just outside the door. It was Link Brady, the sheriff. The coincidence of having just been exposed by the deputy sheriff and now finding the sheriff, apparently waiting for him, nettled Corbett.

He said to Brady, "That deputy of yours has a big mouth."

"He's got more than that," replied the sheriff easily. "He's got a fast gun."

"There's always someone somewhere who's faster with a gun. And sooner or later they meet."

Brady grinned up at Corbett. "He spill that you were a detective?"

Corbett nodded. "Where'd he learn that?"

"Search me. Eben's got his own sources of information. He's pretty close-mouthed about such things and I don't usually question him. As far as I'm concerned he's a good deputy sheriff."

"I'm surprised you'd put a badge on a man with his reputation."

"Oh, I gave it a lot of thought and I talked to some of the —the big people around here. The way things are right now, they seemed to think it might not be a bad idea to have a lawman who could stand up to the kind of people that've been comin' in here, on their own terms. Which reminds me, I want to have a few words with you. This morning you led me to believe that you were one of them. You didn't tell me that Sam Forest had sent for you because you were a detective."

"I work for a man named Jarvis in Chicago," said Corbett. "I take my orders from him and his orders were to keep it a secret."

"Sure," said Brady. "You'd come and told me that, I'd a kept it to myself and I'd probably been able to make Smith keep his mouth shut." He got to his feet. "You figure maybe it might be a good idea to cooperate with the sheriff's office?"

"No," said Corbett, "I don't."

"Suit yourself. You get into trouble, you're on your own." The sheriff nodded curtly to Corbett and walked away, heading across the street to his office.

It had been Corbett's intention to go to his room and go to

28

bed early, but he found himself too irritated to do so and after standing in front of the hotel, he shrugged and started back down the street. He passed the saloon and saw that the lights were on in Brady's store.

Though the window he could see Cathy Brady seated behind the counter reading a book. He opened the door and went into the store.

Cathy looked up from her book. "Oh, hello," she said brightly. "Want some more stamps on the special deal?"

"I've got enough to last me awhile. You keep the store open every night?"

"Until nine o'clock, although I don't usually work here. But Wednesday night is Dad's night for poker so I watch the place. I haven't had a customer in twenty minutes." She suddenly assumed a frown. "I forgot, I'm mad at you."

"Mad? Why?"

"This afternoon when we played the guessing game about your job, you didn't tell me you were a detective."

"News travels fast in this town," said Corbett. "How long have you known?"

"Oh, let's see, when did I say the last customer was in here? Twenty minutes ago. That's when I heard it."

"Who was your last customer?"

"The deputy sheriff. He bought a sack of Bull Durham."

"He keeps crowding me," said Corbett. "He isn't going to be able to smoke. At least not with his mouth."

"You're going to shut it for him? A real rough one, aren't you? But you don't know much about our deputy sheriff. He doesn't fight with his fists. He's a gun fighter, one of the best they say, or is it the worst, when it's a gun fighter?"

Corbett made a gesture of dismissal. "You're not working tomorrow night, are you?"

"No."

"You've had time to think about it," said Corbett. "What about that date?"

She shook her head. "Maybe some places, like Chicago, perhaps a detective is a respectable citizen. But not here."

"I know," said Corbett. "This is where they make a gun fighter a deputy sheriff."

Cathy closed her book with a bang. "It's nine o'clock, time to close up."

"My bedtime, I guess," said Corbett ruefully.

"Good night, Mr. Corbett."

"The name is Jim."

"I'll think about it."

Chapter Six

His room was already lit up by the rising sun when Corbett awakened, having gone to bed early the night before. He found his watch lying beside the bed and saw that it was only a few minutes after five. There was no use getting up this early. The town was still asleep.

He lay in bed thinking of the things he should do that day. The revealing of his identity did not worry him too much. It might even work out for the best. He had been a detective for three years. Sometimes his identity was known when he went to work on a case, sometimes it was kept a secret. In this particular case, Corbett would have preferred that it not be known, but he did not believe that he would be irreparably harmed.

He wondered what one of the people in Seven Oaks would think when she learned that he was a detective instead of a gun fighter with a record of multiple killings. Actually he had merely distorted the truth. Most of what he had told her was basically true, even though boastful.

He was very good at his work. He had never failed on one of his detective assignments and the work he had done prior to becoming a detective—well, he was alive. That proved he had been good at it.

Before six o'clock Corbett was up. He poured water into the cracked washbowl and shaved himself. Then he took off his heavy Army undershirt and washed himself to his waist. He dressed slowly and by six-fifteen was descending to the hotel lobby. A clerk who was on duty told Corbett that the dining room was open, had been since six o'clock.

An elderly storekeeper was at one side of the room having his breakfast. Corbett sat down at a table just inside the door. He ordered ham and eggs with potatoes. He ate it and washed it down with coffee and felt unsatisfied. He signaled to the waitress and ordered a stack of flannel cakes and a second cup of coffee.

"I've got to charge you for two breakfasts," the girl said. "A dollar altogether."

"That's all right with me," said Corbett.

The girl went off and Bonner, the Wells Fargo agent, came in and moved to the table. "All right if I join you?"

"Suit yourself."

Bonner sat down. "That—what Eben Smith said last night about you being a detective—it's true?"

Corbett shrugged. "Does it worry you?"

"I'm not happy about it," admitted the worried-looking express agent.

"Been tapping the till?"

Bonner exclaimed in anguish, "That's a terrible thing to say to a man!"

"It is," said Corbett, "if it isn't true . . ."

"It's not," cried Bonner. "It's not really. Sometimes when I get a little short I, uh, draw a little money against my wages . . ."

"Oh," said Corbett. Then, "Does the company know you draw against them?"

"Not really. I mean, no. They—they wouldn't approve of it."

"That reminds me," said Corbett. "I believe you owe me twenty-one dollars."

Bonner's face revealed the fact that he was very unhappy about that and had come prepared to talk about it. "Could you wait until the first? It's only a few days . . ."

"Eleven days."

"I—I'm pretty short this month."

"How short?"

"A hundred dollars. A little more maybe . . ."

"How much more?"

Bonner gulped. "As a matter of fact it's over two hundred."

"How much does Wells Fargo pay you?"

"Six—sixty dollars a month."

"Mister," said Corbett, "you *are* in trouble. You've drawn three months' pay in advance." He looked sharply at Bonner. "That is, if you've told me everything."

"I was short two hundred last month," groaned Bonner. "I told the company I didn't collect from one of our big customers. They insist I collect this month."

"The store? Brady's?"

"No. One of the ranchers. The Widow Hubbard."

"But she *did* pay?"

Bonner nodded dumbly.

The waitress came with Corbett's second breakfast. She

looked inquiringly at Bonner. The express agent said, "I'll just have a cup of coffee."

"Get something to eat, man," said Corbett. "It'll make you feel better."

"I'm not really hungry."

"Bring him this," said Corbett, indicating his order.

The waitress went off and Corbett began eating. Bonner watched him awhile. Finally he nerved himself up to asking the crucial question.

"Are you here—investigating me?"

Corbett chuckled. "I *thought* that was what was bothering you. No, I'm not working for Wells Fargo."

"Eben said the Forests brought you here. But I—I thought maybe that was just a cover-up."

"It isn't," said Corbett. Then, "You seem to be in with the people in town. If you had to make a smart guess who would you say bushwhacked Sam Forest?"

Bonner sent a quick, uneasy look over his shoulder. "I wouldn't be smart if I tried to guess. In fact it would be about the dumbest thing a man in this town could do."

"Be dumb then."

"Not me, Corbett, not me. I've been in this town three years and I've seen this thing building up. It's a power struggle and I'm not going to get sucked into it. There are too many people with guns who don't mind using them. Ain't that why you're here?"

"It's a job of work with me, that's all."

"It ain't *my* work."

"What is your work?" asked Corbett. "Playing poker?"

"I'm through. I've had it," said Bonner fervently. "I'm never going to sit in another poker game . . ."

"Until tonight. You're four hundred dollars in the hole. You're going to try to get even . . ."

"No, I'm not. I've had my lesson."

"I won a hundred dollars last night," said Corbett, "in one hand. Four hands like that would square you up."

"I know, but the way my luck's running—" Bonner shook his head.

Corbett said, "That hundred I won last night. How'd you like to have it?"

"I'd like it fine," said Bonner. Then his eyes narrowed. "How do you mean?"

"I need information," said Corbett. "Information a stranger can't get, especially a detective. But it's information you probably already know."

"Like what?"

32

"Like how many gun fighters have been brought into this country in the last three months. How many and who brought them?"

Bonner stared at Corbett. "What you're asking me to do is be a spy for you?"

"No," said Corbett, "I'm offering you a chance to earn a hundred dollars. You could get lucky tonight if you had a good enough stake."

It was, of course, the right appeal to make to a compulsive gambler. A hundred dollars would not cover Bonner's shortage with his company, but it would enable him to make a fresh onslaught against his card-playing companions. It was found money.

He said, "What about the twenty-one I owe you?"

"That's extra," said Corbett, "a bonus."

"Slip it to me under the table," said Bonner in a low voice.

Corbett took out a sheaf of folded bills, counted a hundred, then added two dollars, which he separated from the hundred, and dropped on the table to pay for his double breakfast as well as Bonner's.

He found Bonner's grasping hand under the table and gave him the money. "You can get the information today?" he asked.

"I think so. Link Brady's been keepin' tabs on the new men coming to Seven Oaks. He splits with Eben Smith on the wanted ones."

"This Smith's turned bounty hunter," observed Corbett. "There are places where *he'd* be picked up for the reward money."

Reinforced with the hundred dollars, Bonner's attitude had become cheerful. "In my business I've learned a lot about outlaws. With half of them the difference is having a job, or not. As long as a man has a job he stays honest . . ."

"Not always," Corbett reminded pointedly.

Bonner scowled. "If he's out of work, he looks for the easy dollar." The scowl remained on his face.

Corbett finished his coffee, pushed back his chair. "I'll see you later, Bonner."

He left the dining room and crossed the street to the livery stable which adjoined the courthouse and sheriff's office. He had taken his horse there the evening before. It was nicely curried this morning and had eaten a good breakfast of oats. At least the liveryman assured him of that.

"A dollar," the man told Corbett.

"I expect to be here a few days," said Corbett. "I'll pay you before I leave."

"Uh-uh," said the liveryman. "You pay me every day." He

added meaningly, "I know who you are. You get yourself bushwhacked and I'm holding the bag."

Corbett grinned and gave the man a silver dollar. He mounted and rode out of the stable. He jogged easily out of town headed for the Forest Ranch.

Chapter Seven

Barney McCorkle was at the corral with a hand who called himself Hardee, after the Confederate general of that name, when he saw Corbett riding up. Under another name Hardee was wanted in both Idaho and Montana.

"That's the Chicago detective," McCorkle exclaimed. "The dirty bastard! I'll give you a hundred out of my own pocket if you get him."

Hardee showed interest. He had once killed a man for two dollars and fifty cents. McCorkle started forward as Corbett dismounted.

"You got a nerve comin' here," he snapped at Corbett.

"I'm working for Miss Julie and Mrs. Forest," replied Corbett. "If *they* want me to talk to you, I'll do it. But until then . . ."

"That's big talk," interposed Hardee, the gun fighter. "Where I come from, man talks like that he's got to back it up."

"Where's that?" snapped Corbett. Then his eyes narrowed as he sized up Hardee. "Don't tell me—let me guess. Montana! I ran into a dirty bushwhacker there one time—his name was Fickett and he looked a hell of a lot like you . . ."

Hardee's mouth opened, remained wide for a moment, then closed.

Corbett sneered at the gunman, "Well, Fickett?"

Hardee, born Fickett, shook his head.

Corbett said, "What was the reward for you in Montana, Fickett? Five hundred? I know some people'd sell their mothers for five hundred dollars. You, for instance. And Eben Smith, Link Brady's deputy."

Corbett waited a moment for Hardee to reply, or make his play, but when he did not he turned his back deliberately on the two men and started toward the house. He was surprised to see Mrs. Forest standing on the door stoop. She apparently had witnessed the scene between Corbett and her foreman and gun-fighter hand.

" 'Morning, ma'am," said Corbett. "My name's Corbett."

"I know," said Mrs. Forest. "Won't you come in?"

35

"Thank you."

Corbett took off his hat and followed Mrs. Forest into the house.

Near the corral McCorkle turned on his gunhand. "So you're chicken, after all!"

Hardee-Fickett scowled at McCorkle. "I'm careful, that's what. That fella's the roughest, toughest son-of-a-bitch in the whole Army."

"Army!"

"That's what he was in Montana," replied Hardee. "He was wearin' a blue suit with big yellow stripes on his sleeves. Sergeant Corbett of the Ninth Cavalry. I seen him clean out a saloon one time all by hisself. Killed one man, crippled two more and cracked a coupla heads."

"All right, he can fight with his hands," snapped McCorkle. "But you've got a gun . . ."

"So's he," retorted Hardee. "And he just happens to be the best shot in the Army. Even when he was in uniform he never wore a regulation holster and he's got that gun of his filed down to a hair trigger."

Corbett sat in the small parlor, which was immaculately clean, and was ill at ease with Mrs. Forest. It was she who had to lead into the subject. "Having been married to Sam Forest for more than twenty-five years, I know pretty well how he thought about most things. They called him a curly wolf, I know, but he actually hated fighting. But he said over and over that a man had to walk straight and look every man in the eye and he couldn't do that if he didn't fight. Life, he said, wasn't worth living if you had to be afraid all the time. He had a strong feeling of ownership. If a man worked for something, it was his and no one had a right to something he did not work for."

"I agree with that, ma'am," said Corbett. "I've been on my own since I was fourteen and I've worked for everything I ever got."

Mrs. Forest went on, "He was a good husband and father." She hesitated and her voice dropped. "He was not entirely happy about the relationship between our foreman and Julie, although he thought that Julie should make that choice by herself without influence."

"I've made it," said Julie, coming out of an adjoining room. "I broke with Barney last night."

She was wearing a house wrapper of a deep red color that may have heightened the color of her cheeks.

"I'm sorry, Julie," said Mrs. Forest, "I didn't think you'd hear. I felt that Mr. Corbett should know everything that might even slightly help him in his work."

36

"It's all right, Mother," said Julie, although her tone did not quite indicate that. She turned to Corbett. "Can I get you a cup of coffee?"

"No, thanks, I had a good breakfast before I rode out." Corbett cleared his throat. "McCorkle's leaving the ranch?"

The two men exchanged a quick look, then Mrs. Forest replied, "The subject hasn't come up. I know that my husband considered him a good foreman . . ."

"My breaking with him has nothing to do with his work," said Julie quickly. "As long as he minds his own business . . ."

"I shouldn't have asked the question," said Corbett. "Except that I may be spending quite a lot of time on the ranch and I don't want to have a fight with him every time I run into him."

"He knows you're a detective," said Mrs. Forest. "He'll be told to cooperate with you."

Corbett nodded and got to his feet. "Just one thing more, ma'am. Am I right in assuming that your husband's relationship with the Holdermans was not—ah—good?"

Tartness came into Mrs. Forest's voice. "They're thieves and outlaws, the lot of them . . ."

"Not Tracy," interposed Julie quickly.

"No, I'm sorry," said Mrs. Forest, "my husband thought well of Tracy. But Pete and those cubs of his, Pete Jr. and Quincy, they actually had the nerve to come here yesterday to the funeral. The truth is that it was probably one of them who—who killed Sam."

"I don't think we should say that, Mother," said Julie worriedly. "We have no proof."

"We will have," said Mrs. Forest firmly. "You'll get it, Mr. Corbett. I'm sure you will. The Holdermans are hand in glove with the outlaws in the badlands and that's the way the cattle have been going. The sheriff won't go into the mountains. Doesn't dare. Then neither does anyone else. But the Holdermans are in and out all the time. They used to live there in fact. They didn't come down until after we had settled here."

"I'm planning to go to the Holderman Ranch from here," said Corbett, smiling thinly. "Is it—safe?"

"I wouldn't advise it," said Mrs. Forest.

Julie shook her head. "Nonsense, Mother. They wouldn't shoot anyone in broad daylight. Not in their own front yard. They aren't *that* brazen. Especially right now."

Mrs. Forest still frowned, however. "I think you should tell them, when you see them, that—that we know you were going there."

37

"I might do that," said Corbett. He nodded. "Thank you, Mrs. Forest." He bowed to Julie. "Miss Julie."

"Julie, call me Julie."

Corbett smiled and took his departure.

Outside, he looked around. McCorkle and his henchman had gone off, although there were two or three hands inside the corral, where there were half a dozen horses.

Corbett was nearing the main east and south road when he saw a pair of riders coming toward him from the range beyond the road. He reached the road and waited.

The riders came on, pulling up abruptly on the south side of the road, but not coming onto it. One of the men was a shifty-eyed youngster in his early twenties. The other sat tall in the saddle, a rugged, handsome-looking man of about forty. It was the tall one who spoke.

"Didn't I see you at the H-Bar-H yesterday?"

"H-Bar-H?"

"The Hubbard Ranch." The man gestured. "This is Hubbard range up to here." He pointed to the west. "And about a mile that way."

"Yes," said Corbett, "I was at the ranch yesterday. I talked to Mrs. Hubbard."

"About what?"

"Ask her," said Corbett. "Maybe she'll tell you."

"I'm Briggs, her foreman," the tall man said crisply. "This is open range, but we don't welcome strangers on it."

"Then you ought to put up signs," retorted Corbett. "Or better yet, fence it in."

"We're thinking of that now," said the foreman. "Wasn't for the cost we'd probably do it."

"Then you'd have yourself a real range war," said Corbett. "Like they're having over in Texas."

"There's something they *haven't* got in Texas—rustlers!"

"No? It's only three years ago that the Adjutant General put out the crime book which listed eight thousand known outlaws in Texas. A lot of them were eating stolen beef and what they couldn't eat they drove over into New Mexico."

"They haven't got eight thousand wanted men now," declared the foreman of the H-Bar-H Ranch. "McNelly's Rangers have gotten rid of more than half of them—and not many of them were fetched in to stand trial." He pointed off to the mountain range in the West. "Some of those that got away from Texas are hiding out there." He scowled. "Those that didn't stop off with the Holdermans. You may even find some friends of yours with Old Pete."

"What kind of a crack is that?"

"You were at the ranch yesterday looking for a job. The

38

widow didn't hire you. And now you've just come from the Forests. Where else can you go except to the Holdermans?"

Corbett shook his head, made a clucking sound with his mouth and, turning his horse, set off westward on the road in the direction of the Holderman Ranch.

The H-Bar-H men watched him a moment or two, then turned their horses and went off at a gallop.

Corbett jogged along at an easy gait. After a few miles, a road that was little more than a trail wound off the main road which, incidentally, had become poorer after leaving the Forest turn-off. A board was nailed to a tree, on which was crudely lettered: TRACY HOLDERMAN.

Corbett rode into the trail-road. He had gone along it for about a mile when he crested a low ridge and saw the layout of Tracy Holderman.

Corbett's first thought was of Cathy Brady. If she married the "good" Holderman and came out here to live with him, she would find the going rather hard.

The "ranch" building layout consisted of a house, a shed and a small corral. The house could be called that only because someone lived in it. It was actually no more than a log cabin chinked with mud. It was scarcely nine by twelve feet in size.

The immediate surroundings, however, were clean. There was sawed and split wood piled up beside the shed.

There was no one in sight as Corbett rode up. "Anyone home?" he called loudly.

Tracy Holderman came out of the log cabin. His sleeves were rolled up and he was wearing a checked apron that was clean.

"Sorry," he said, "didn't hear you ride up. Been doin' the breakfast dishes."

"What you need is a wife," said Corbett easily.

The remark did not please Tracy. "Look, Mister," he said, "I haven't got time for visitin'. Unless you got business here . . ."

"Just a neighborly call," said Corbett.

"Neighborly, hell," said Tracy. "You were shining up to Cathy yesterday and you're here to see how poor I live. Probably so you could make something of it with Cathy. This is a one-man spread. I do all the work myself. I built this house with my own hands. I haven't got any money in the bank, but I own eighty head of stock. What've you got—outside of a fast gun?"

Corbett put his hands together and clapped a couple of times. "Very good, Tracy, very good."

Tracy's face had turned a deep red in spite of his sun tan. "You like to make a man small, don't you, Corbett?"

"Not necessarily, Tracy. If it'll make you feel better, I took the wrong turn in the road. I was on my way to your family's spread."

"Naturally," said Tracy bitterly. "They're your kind. The old man'll probably hire you."

"Wait a minute, Tracy!" exclaimed Corbett. "Weren't you in town last night?"

"You saw me in the store. I went home from there."

"Then you're probably the only man in this area who doesn't know I was exposed last night by Deputy Sheriff Smith. I thought everybody in the valley knew it by now. I'm a detective."

A gasp was torn from Tracy Holderman's throat. "A detective!"

"I was hired by Sam Forest. He had an idea that someone was trying to kill him. As it turned out, he was right. I didn't get here until yesterday, but the family wants me to stay on —and find the man who killed Forest."

"And that's why you're on your way to the family's place?" cried Tracy.

"It seemed like a good place to start."

"They'll kill you," blurted out Tracy. "If they know you're a detective you'll never leave the ranch alive."

"Well," said Corbett, "if anyone knows your father and brothers, it's you."

"That's why I left them," cried Tracy. "Don't you see—I didn't want any part of their—their way of life."

"You *bought* this ranch?" asked Corbett.

Tracy blinked twice. "No, I got it from my father. It's just a sliver, less than two hundred acres. It's the only thing I got from the family and I figured I was entitled to that much. I was on'y twenty when I settled here. That was eight years ago." He felt it necessary to add sharply, "I started with three head of cattle that I bought and paid for. I've had to sell a few steers now and then to keep goin', but I'm building up my herd all the time. I'll make out."

"I think you will," said Corbett. He nodded to the good Holderman. "See you."

"I warned you, remember," exclaimed Tracy. "Don't go over there."

Corbett grinned. "I'll warn *you*, Tracy. Put a bridle on that girl of yours before someone grabs her away. Someone like me . . ."

He kneed his horse and the animal took off at a gallop. He did not look back at Tracy Holderman.

40

Chapter Eight

Alice Hubbard came out of the store, carrying a brown paper bag filled with purchases. She was followed by Cathy Brady carrying a similar sack. They took them to the buckboard and deposited them carefully on the floorboard.

Cathy flashed a smile at the older woman. "Thank you, Mrs. Hubbard." She started to turn away, but Alice Hubbard stopped her.

"A man came out to see me yesterday. He's a stranger in town . . ."

"You mean the detective?"

"Detective?" asked Alice Hubbard, startled.

"Yes—he was in the store. He's got a great line—tried to make a date with me. Only I wasn't having any of it." She stopped, "Why do you ask, Mrs. Hubbard?"

"He asked me for a job. I—well, frankly, I thought your father might have heard something about him from his brother, the sheriff."

"He fooled Uncle Link, I guess," said Cathy. "Pretending to be a gun fighter hired by Sam Forest. But Eben Smith, Uncle Link's deputy, exposed him last night. Dad was there at the time. It's all over town by now. It seems he's here to try to find out who killed Sam Forest." She stopped. "Uncle Link wasn't the only one fooled by him. *I* thought he was a gun fighter too. I mean, there've been so many of them lately." She stopped again, disconcerted. "I'm sorry, Mrs. Hubbard."

"Nothing to be sorry about, Cathy. I've hired gunhands. What else could I do, with the Holdermans and Sam Forest bringing them in? You've got to fight fire with fire. And being a woman, I've got to have twice as much fire, or they'd burn me to a crisp. I've lost more than a thousand head of cattle in the last six months."

"I know," said Cathy, frowning. "It's a terrible thing. And now they've started killing." She winced, then, to get off the immediate topic, made a quick, wild switch. "What did you think of the—the detective?"

41

"I didn't know he was a detective. I was thinking of him as a gun fighter when I talked to him."

"That's how *I* thought of him. Except that he—he talked so well. Much better than any of the other cowhands and—well, I thought him a rather striking man. A—a strong man."

"He's that," said Alice Hubbard thoughtfully. "He may even be a very good detective . . ."

A little shudder ran through Cathy. "But a detective! Makes my skin crawl. He was pretending to be one thing and all the time he was, well, detecting!"

"He's working for the Forests?" asked Mrs. Hubbard.

"Yes. I don't know how straight this is, but the story is that he was actually hired by Mr. Forest, only by the time he arrived here, Mr. Forest had been mur—killed. But Julie came to town last night and said that her mother wants Mr. Corbett—if that's his real name—to stay here and arrest the —murderer." She shook her head. "I think he's going to waste his time, now that everyone knows he's a detective."

Alice Hubbard nodded thoughtfully and untwisted the lines from about the whip. She climbed into the buckboard, then suddenly smiled at Cathy. "How are things progressing between you and Tracy?"

"Oh, *that!*" exclaimed Cathy. "That reminds me—this detective, he joked about that. Kept calling Tracy the *good* Holderman. Is that the way people talk about him?"

"It's a good description, isn't it?" asked Alice Hubbard.

"Then you *have* heard it?"

Alice Hubbard nodded. "Don't let it bother you, Cathy. You're not engaged to a family, you know . . ."

"But I'm *not* engaged!"

Alice Hubbard pretended mock surprise. "Then there's something wrong with that young man. Perhaps he should be called the *bashful*, or the *slow* Holderman." She suddenly slapped the rumps of her team of horses with the lines. "Goodbye, Cathy!"

She drove off, going through the town of Seven Oaks. She soon reached the road that turned left to her ranch, but she did not make the turn. She continued straight ahead.

She put the team into a fast trot that ate up the distance. She was at the Forest Ranch in little more than a half hour after leaving Seven Oaks.

As she climbed down from the buckboard, Julie Forest came out of the house. "Mrs. Hubbard," she exclaimed. "How good of you to come."

"Just thought I'd pay my respects to your mother," said Mrs. Hubbard. "But I won't bother her if she's not up to it."

Julie sent a quick look over her shoulder, then came closer.

"I wish you *would* talk to her awhile, Mrs. Hubbard. It'll do her good."

"Very well, Julie."

Alice Hubbard went into the house, where Mrs. Forest was working in the kitchen. She seemed glad to see Mrs. Hubbard and insisted that they go into the front room where Julie brought a tray with coffee and cups in a few minutes.

"It's been so long since we've had company," said Mrs. Forest, "I've almost forgotten how to act."

That was as close as she got to talking about the recent tragedy that had befallen her. During the rest of the fifteen minutes that Mrs. Hubbard remained with her, they talked of other things, the weather, the grass, the problems of running a ranch, the household work.

Julie had been right. When Alice Hubbard entered the house Mrs. Forest was in a depressed mood. When she left she was considerably more cheerful.

"If you feel like it," said Alice Hubbard as she went to the door, "drive over any time. I'm never so busy I can't sit down and have a cup of coffee. In fact I'm always looking for an excuse."

She left the house and Julie followed her out. "Thank you, Mrs. Hubbard," she said, "for coming by."

"Persuade her to come over tomorrow," said Alice Hubbard. She got into the buckboard and picked up the lines. "Oh—I was in Seven Oaks. There's all sorts of idle talk there about the—the detective you've hired."

Julie showed annoyance. "He was out here this morning. Early. Barney McCorkle had to shoot off his mouth in town last night. He had a fight with Mr. Corbett—that's the detective." She added spitefully, "And I don't think Barney feels very good today. He got licked."

"He was out to see me yesterday, this Corbett," said Alice Hubbard. "He pretended to be a gun fighter looking for a job."

"Oh, that was going to be his—his cover," exclaimed Julie. "Dad sent for him, but he didn't want people to know he was a detective." She gnawed at her lower lip. "I guess he should have sent for him sooner."

"You can't look back, Julie," said Mrs. Hubbard. "You can't say I should have done this, or that. You do the best you can at the time. Perhaps it's the wrong thing, but if you've done a thing you've got to live with it. You can't spend all your time moaning over your mistakes, or regretting them."

"That's the way Dad used to talk," exclaimed Julie. "Mother told me a story about him last night. Years ago, not

43

long after we settled here, there were some rustlers who kept stealing from us. There was no sheriff here then, no law of any kind. Dad and some men caught the rustlers and they hanged two of them. He felt terribly bad about it, but he said it was the only thing they could have done—at the time. He said rustlers knew that they would be hanged if they were caught and when they went into it they gambled with their lives." She stopped. "It stopped the rustling, I understand."

"I know," said Mrs. Hubbard. "That happened right after we settled here. My husband was one of the men with your father." She exhaled heavily, flashed a smile at Julie. "Come and visit me with your mother. Or alone, if you feel like it."

"I'll do that, Mrs. Hubbard," said Julie. "I—I sometimes feel the need of talking to somebody. I mean, somebody besides Mother."

Chapter Nine

Corbett tested the mechanics of his Winchester rifle at some distance from the Holderman Ranch, and, as he neared it, slid his revolver in and out of the holster to make sure that it was working smoothly. He slowed his horse to an easy walk so that it would be ready for a burst of speed if it was necessary to make a quick getaway from the ranch.

He saw the ranch headquarters from a distance of a half-mile. There was a frame house that had once been painted, but had not had any paint now in some years. There were at least a dozen other buildings clustered around it—bunkhouses, barns, sheds. There were haystacks and a couple of big corrals.

There was much activity around the ranch, some cowboys breaking broncs in one of the corrals, others performing various chores.

Pete Holderman sat on a rocking chair on the porch of the house, which Corbett could now see had been badly neglected. The surroundings about the good Holderman's tiny ranch were clean, well kept up; here disorderliness was the rule. There were tin cans, bottles on the ground, bits and chunks of old harness. Bridles, long rotted, were spread over the porch rails, or hanging from nails in the wall.

Pete was in his late fifties, a grizzled barrel of a man. At one time he had probably weighed two hundred and fifty pounds. He had lost some weight as he got older, but he was still a big man with a huge chest. And a stomach that had once been hard as the barrel of a horse.

A younger edition of Pete Holderman was coming from one of the bunkhouses as Corbett rode up. He stopped abruptly when he saw Corbett.

The elder Pete Holderman called to Corbett, "Howdy, stranger, light and rest awhile."

His offspring snapped, "What the hell do you want?"

Corbett dismounted. He ignored the younger Holderman. "Name's Corbett," he called to Pete Senior. "Like to talk to you."

"Sure thing. Corbett, did you say?" Then Pete leaned for-

45

ward in his rocking chair. "Hey, you're the fella was at Sam Forest's funeral yesterday." He smirked. "I told Sam years ago I'd come to his funeral. He always expected it'd be the other way 'round . . ."

Young Pete suddenly moved. He came forward, planted himself before Corbett, in between Corbett and Pete Senior.

"I asked you a question," he said in a half-snarl. "I didn't get no answer. What the hell do you want?"

"Mind your manners," retorted Corbett. "Your father's talking to me . . ."

"Reach," said a voice behind Corbett. "And if you make a play, I don't mind. I wouldn't mind a-tall!"

It was the voice of Quincy Holderman, who had talked to Corbett at the Forest Ranch the day before. Corbett had walked into it with his eyes wide open. He had been distracted by the elder Holderman's folksy greeting, the belligerence of the Holderman directly in front of him. The third Holderman had been able to come up behind him.

He was fairly caught. It would be suicide to make a play. He raised his hands to shoulder height.

"Higher!" snapped Quincy.

Corbett reached for as much sky as he could grab.

"Get the artillery, Pete," ordered Quincy, behind Corbett.

Pete Junior moved first to the horse and whipped out the rifle from the saddle scabbard. He threw it in the general direction of the porch. Then he moved up beside Corbett and snatched the revolver from its holster. He spun it after the rifle.

On the porch Pete Senior got to his feet. He came down the two-step flight of stairs. "Always did want to see me another detective." He chuckled as he came toward Corbett and his sons. "Last time I saw one was right after the war. One of Billy Pinkerton's boys. He was lookin' for a bank robber, he said, and thought he might be up there—" Pete gestured to the mountains over his shoulder beyond the house and the range. "Don't think he ever come out." He stopped a few feet from Corbett and sized him up carefully. "Mmm, big, all right, but not much muscle in them bones."

"He's one of the lean ones," chortled Pete Junior.

"Could be. You work for Billy Pinkerton, son?" asked Old Pete.

"No," replied Corbett shortly.

"That's all right, you don't *have* to talk if you don't want to. You're here to get the fellas bushwhacked old Sam Forest, hey? So you naturally come out here figgerin' we done the job." He held up a cautioning finger. "Not that the idea ain't

46

a good one, mind you. Only we didn't do it. I mourned Old Sam yesterday, but that was yesterday and today's today."

"You want we should work him over, Paw?" asked Quincy, who was a bit smaller than his brother, but evidently of a meaner disposition. Which was hard to believe.

"I'm thinkin' about it, Quincy," said Old Pete. "Just like to get some more information from the detective first."

"You'll get nothing from me," snapped Corbett.

"That's what the Pinkerton man said," replied Old Pete, "right after the war. Mmm, must be fourteen-fifteen years ago." He nodded. "Old Sam Forest was a real curly wolf, the meanest, orneriest sonofabitch in this country. I whupped him once when he first came here, but it didn't discourage him none a-tall. Yes sir, a real tough sonofabitch. Only one man tougher in this whole danged country. Me. Take hold of him, Quincy. You too, Pete."

Quincy came up from behind, grabbed Corbett's left arm in both of his. Pete, moving in from the other side, grabbed not only Corbett's right arm, but snaked his left about Corbett's head, getting the forearm under the chin and practically cutting off Corbett's breath.

"Hate to do this, Corbett," said old Pete, his cheerfulness belying his words. "But I made me some rules years ago. One was don't have nothin' to do with lawmen. Now I know you ain't a real sure-enough lawman, bein' only a detective, but my second rule was don't let any goddam detective set foot on your land. It ain't . . ."

He broke off in the middle of the sentence and drove his right fist into the pit of Corbett's stomach. He had a lot of power yet in his old muscles and bones, and a gasp was torn from Corbett's throat that could not even clear the channel because of Pete Junior's forearm.

Old Pete stepped back and peered into Corbett's face. He shook his head. "That's the trouble, a man gets old he loses his strength. Hell, I knocked out Billy Pinkerton's man with one punch and here you are, still kicking." He stepped forward and drove his left fist into Corbett's stomach.

There wasn't quite as much zing to the second blow as the first one, but it did the trick. Corbett sagged in the arms of the younger Holdermans. Quincy released his hold, stepped around and smashed his fist into Corbett's face.

Young Pete let go of him then and Quincy picked him up. Young Pete promptly knocked him down again, then he picked him up and Quincy hit Corbett. They played the game back and forth, but it got to be too much trouble after awhile, picking Corbett up and holding him up so the other man could hit him.

When Corbett was completely unconscious his body was too limp to hold up and they let him lie on the ground. That didn't stop them from kicking him, however.

Old Pete said, "I guess that's about enough, boys."

What he really meant was that he wanted to kick Corbett himself, and he gave him a couple of good ones in the ribs.

"I guess that'll take care of the detectives for awhile," he said cheerfully.

"I hope not," said Quincy.

Old Pete called to one of the hands who had gathered nearby to watch the proceedings. "You, Grimes, fetch a bucket of water."

The hand caught up a wooden bucket near a cattle trough, filled it with water and trotted up. He dumped the entire bucketful on Corbett, who twitched and kicked once.

"Want me to carry him to the trough and dump him in?" asked the hand.

"Leave him be," said Old Pete. "He'll come around after awhile."

But Corbett lay motionless for ten minutes. Old Pete then talked to his worthy sons and the latter lifted Corbett into the saddle of his horse. They let his upper body fall forward onto the horse's neck and tied a lasso about the body to hold it in the saddle. They drew the rope tight and knotted it, then kicked Corbett's horse so that it started off at a wild gallop.

Chapter Ten

It was Sheriff Link Brady who found the still unconscious Corbett. He had passed the turn-off to Tracy Holderman's place but was still some three miles from the main Holderman Ranch when he saw the horse coming toward him. At first Brady thought it was a riderless horse, but when he saw the man lying across the saddle pommel, he sent his horse swiftly toward it and, catching the bridle of Corbett's horse, dismounted.

He cut the rope that bound Corbett and eased him to the ground. It was not until Corbett was stretched out on his back that Brady recognized him. He exclaimed aloud.

"Damn fool!"

He went to his horse and took down the canteen that he always carried when he rode out of the town of Seven Oaks. He spilled some water on Corbett's face and dabbed at the swollen, bruised features with a big bandanna handkerchief.

A low moan issued from Corbett's lips, his eyes fluttered, then blinked and finally focused upon Brady's face.

"Who did it?" asked the sheriff. "Who beat you up?"

Corbett remained mute.

Brady dabbed again at Corbett's face with his wet handkerchief. "Like some water?" he asked.

Corbett barely nodded. Brady slipped his arm under Corbett's head, raised it a few inches and put the canteen to his lips. Corbett swallowed a mouthful of water, choked and sputtered moisture into Brady's face. Brady did not seem to mind. He waited until the coughing stopped, then again put the canteen to Corbett's mouth. Corbett drank this time and seemed refreshed.

Brady raised him to a sitting position but kept his arm behind the shoulders. Corbett drank again from the canteen.

Brady replaced the cap on the canteen.

"The Holdermans?" he asked.

Corbett still made no reply. Brady said, "Hear you licked McCorkle last night. Barney can hold his own against any of the Holdermans."

"All three of them?" asked Corbett. "At the same time?"

49

Brady let out a wheeze. "I saw you ride out this morning. You were wearing a six-gun and a Winchester. They take your guns?"

"I'll get them back," said Corbett, "next time."

"If you go out there again it'll be the last time," snorted Brady. "Old Pete and his boys have caused me more trouble than anybody since I've worn a badge. He's got a half-dozen people out here that I know are wanted somewhere, but I've never yet gotten one of them into the lockup." He shook his head. "Seven Oaks is no place for a detective, Corbett. Jarvis doesn't pay you enough for you to get yourself killed and that's what's going to happen if you stay here. My advice to you is give it up, go back to Chicago."

"I will," said Corbett, "after you've hung the man who murdered Sam Forest."

"If I had an army," said Brady, "or a company of Texas Rangers, I'd get the man, but since there's only me and a single deputy here, I'm pretty sure I'm never going to put a rope on Sam's murderer." He added sharply, "It ain't that I've got less sand than the next man and if I did have, Eben Smith's faced the worst there ever was. I still wouldn't come out here to the Holdermans and try to take away one of them if he wasn't willing to go with me."

When Corbett's horse stopped before the hitch rail of the Seven Oaks Hotel, Corbett remained in the saddle until Link Brady had dismounted and stepped to his side.

"Just fall against me," said Brady, holding up his hands.

Corbett followed the sheriff's instructions. He leaned sideward and fell into the strong arms of Brady, who moved back and eased him to the ground.

"I'll help you to your room," said Brady after they had moved onto the board sidewalk.

"No," said Corbett, "I'll make it on my own. I can walk."

"I'll send Doc Hudkins over," offered Brady.

"There are no broken bones," said Corbett. "I won't need him."

Gregson opened the hotel door and let out a long, low whistle. "You get stomped by a herd of wild broncs?" he cried.

Corbett walked stiffly past him into the lobby. He made it all right to the staircase, but then had to raise one leg to place it on a stair. It sent an excruciating pain through his body, but then he placed his weight upon the higher step and raised his other foot up to it.

Repeating the process, it took him quite awhile to reach

the head of the stairs, but the last few steps were not as painful as the first.

He got into his room, stepped to the side of the bed and fell upon it. He was still lying in the same position when there was a knock on the door.

"Dr. Hudkins," said a voice outside the room.

Corbett made no reply, but the doctor opened the door and came into the room. He set his bag on the floor and bent over Corbett. He whistled softly.

"I'd hate to see the other man."

"Let me alone," said Corbett.

"Can't," said the doctor. "The sheriff'd run me out of town."

He turned Corbett from his side onto his back, raised his feet up onto the bed, then opened his bag and produced a pair of scissors. He cut the shirt away from Corbett's body, then did the same with the undershirt. He whistled when he saw the battered and bruised torso and began prodding here and there. He produced a few groans from Corbett, but completed his examination.

"You're not going to walk for a few days, but there don't seem to be any broken bones."

He worked over Corbett for more than an hour, washing his torso, dabbing iodine and liniment here and there, putting on a bandage or two and a few pieces of adhesive plaster.

When he was finished he said, "I'll talk to Gregson and have him send up your meals."

"When I'm hungry I'll walk downstairs," said Corbett.

"Then you're going to get awfully hungry." The doctor shook a couple of pills from a bottle, then dropped them back into the bottle. "I'll leave you these pills. Take one every four hours, or whenever something hurts too much."

He had moved the washstand over to the bed and set the bottle on the stand. Then he gathered together his things and picked up his bag.

"I'll stop by this evening and take a look at you. Get some sleep."

When the door was closed, Corbett turned over with an effort and found the pill bottle. He swallowed two of the pills. Five minutes later he was sound asleep.

It was Bonner, the Wells Fargo man, who awakened Corbett. He banged on the door and, when he got no response, opened the door and went in and shook Corbett.

Corbett was awakened by pain darting through him and he groaned and opened his eyes. It was a moment before he recognized Bonner.

"What do you want?"

"I've earned my money," Bonner said. Then he reacted. "Hey, you look like hell. I heard that the Holdermans worked you over, but I didn't think it was that bad."

Corbett made a tremendous effort and sat up on the bed. He had to remain still a moment then before he could reach for the pill bottle. He tossed three of them into his mouth and, crunching them quickly, swallowed them. Then, with another effort, he swung his feet to the floor.

Bonner had stood by watching Corbett. "Now," he said, "the Holdermans hired eight men, fired four, the Forests got in twelve men, fired six, all of them right after Old Sam was killed. The Widow Hubbard—this'll surprise you—she put on fourteen new hands and hasn't fired any of them. She's got more people on her ranch now than either the Forests or the Holdermans, although with the Holdermans you never can tell. They can always whistle down some of the wild ones from the hills. That the information you wanted?"

"I guess so," said Corbett.

"I thought maybe you'd like to make a deal for some other news. Like a telegram a certain party sent today."

"What do you know about telegrams?"

"I'm the telegraph operator. I send every telegram that leaves Seven Oaks and I receive every one that comes in."

"Who sent the telegram?"

"A hundred dollars and I'll show it to you."

Corbett tried to make an impatient gesture of dismissal and found that the effort caused him too much pain. He repeated, "Who sent the telegram?"

"A hundred dollars."

"If it's worth a hundred dollars I'll pay you. If it isn't, the hell with you."

"It's worth it. Pay me first."

"Damn you," swore Corbett, "*I'll* send a telegram. To Wells Fargo's home office and I'll stand over you while you send it."

"You wouldn't know what I sent."

"I could read Morse code before I was seventeen. And I could send a telegraph message."

Bonner hesitated, then scowling drew a crumpled telegram blank from his pocket. Corbett smoothed out the sheet and holding it sidewards so that he could use the waning light coming from the window, read the message. It was addressed to the Secretary of the Interior, Washington, D.C. It read:

Cattle rustling has reached such vast proportions in this area that I respectfully request you issue an order to all Indian

52

agents in the southern part of this state to stop buying beef, unless sold with bona fide bills of sale, and stock brands carefully checked. Indian agents at San Marco, Mobete and Vittorio Reservations should be especially warned and investigated. I have communicated with Governor Walters and he advises that he will make similar formal requests to you.

Alice Hubbard

"Is it worth the hundred?" asked Bonner.

Painfully Corbett reached into his pocket and brought out a sheaf of bills. He counted out five twenties. Bonner snatched them from his hand. His eyes tried to see how much money there was left. His estimate seemed to please him.

"I may have something for you tomorrow," Bonner said as he took his leave.

Corbett nodded. He thought of getting up and going down and having his dinner, but the pills he had just taken were having their effect on him. He dropped back on the bed and in a moment or two was sound asleep again.

Chapter Eleven

It was only eight o'clock in the morning when Julie Forest rode into the town of Seven Oaks. She stopped in front of the hotel and, tying her horse to the hitchrail, went into the hotel.

Gregson had apparently just come on duty.

"What room is Mr. Corbett in?" she asked.

"Five," replied Gregson automatically, then exclaimed as Julie started for the stairs, "Wait—you can't go up to his room!"

Julie stopped at the edge of the stairs. "Why not?"

"Because he's—I mean, it ain't right for a girl to go to a man's hotel room . . ."

"Phooey," said Julie. "He's working for us and he's hurt."

She turned and climbed up the stairs. She had no difficulty finding Room 5 and, reaching it, knocked on the door.

Corbett was awake, but could scarcely move a muscle in his body. The long sleep had stiffened him completely and the pain of his wounds and bruises had become magnified overnight.

He groaned, "Yes, what is it?"

"It's me, Julie Forest," called Julie. "I want to see you . . ."

"Go 'way," Corbett replied.

Julie opened the door. Her exclamation of horror as she caught sight of Corbett could have been heard down in the hotel lobby.

She dropped to her knees before the bed. Her fingers ran quickly over Corbett's face, touching or almost touching all of his bruises and wounds.

"You've got to have a doctor!" she cried.

"He's been here," said Corbett. Then he added bitterly, "He says I'll be all right in about a week."

"You haven't eaten," she said. "I'll get you something . . ."

Corbett started to protest, but Julie was already leaving the room. She went downstairs into the dining room and ordered scrambled eggs, toast and coffee, then as an afterthought added an order of ham.

54

She waited until the food was ready, then carried the tray upstairs. When she got to the room, she found Corbett seated on the edge of the bed. He had somehow put on a clean shirt, although it was not buttoned. She did not know how much effort and agony Corbett had endured to make himself presentable.

Corbett drank the coffee, but did not eat. Julie declared that she would not leave until he had finished the meal.

Rather than argue, Corbett ate some of the scrambled eggs, but the toast was almost too much for him. One of the Holdermans had practically unhinged his jaw muscles and the act of chewing sent excruciating pain through him. He took a couple of his pills and after a moment or two found that the pain had been numbed sufficiently so that he could chew a little better.

Julie gathered up the plates and stacked them on the tray.

"I'll come back in time for your dinner," she promised.

"No!" cried Corbett. "I can manage for myself."

"You were working for us when you were hurt," declared Julie firmly. "The least we can do is see that you're properly taken care of." Her nostrils suddenly flared. "I'm going to see that the sheriff arrests the Holdermans."

"He won't," said Corbett.

"He's *got* to," said Julie fiercely. "I'll swear out a warrant for them."

"Let them alone," exclaimed Corbett. Then seeing that nothing else would deter her, "I want them loose. It's important to—to my investigation . . ."

"It was the Holderman's who killed my father?"

"I don't know. I think so—but I need the proof and if they're arrested I can't get it."

Julie nodded thoughtfully. "We've got as many men working for us as the Holdermans have. If the sheriff needs help . . ."

"Leave the sheriff alone," snapped Corbett. "He's the one who found me and brought me in to town. Besides, he's investigating on his own and you mustn't interfere with him. Not now . . ."

"All right," said Julie reluctantly. "But promise me one thing—don't get up today. Don't even try. I'll be back at twelve o'clock . . ."

Corbett was still protesting when she went out with the tray.

Leaving the hotel, Julie mounted her horse and sent it into an easy canter. She had no intention of going home, however. The ranch of the Widow Hubbard was closer to town and it was there that she went.

55

She found Alice Hubbard in the ranch yard giving orders to her foreman, Briggs. But Mrs. Hubbard came quickly toward her.

"I'm glad you've come, Julie. How is your mother?"

"She's all right," replied Julie. "I didn't really intend to come, but I didn't want to go home, then return to Seven Oaks by twelve o'clock."

"You've already been to town?"

"Yes, I went to see Mr. Corbett, the detective. He went out to the Holderman Ranch yesterday and was terribly beaten."

"He's seriously hurt?" asked Mrs. Hubbard.

"He can hardly move and there's no one to take care of him at the hotel."

"Has Doctor Hudkins been to see him?"

"Yes. Mr. Corbett told me he's been ordered to stay in bed for a week. He's very stubborn, didn't even want to eat breakfast. I—I made him eat."

Alice Hubbard looked thoughtfully at Julie. The girl was unaware that Mrs. Hubbard's restraint was even greater than usual, that she was breathing heavier and trying not to show it.

She said to Julie, "You like this—this detective?"

"*Like* him? What do you mean? He's working for us and the least we can do is see that he's taken care of."

"Of course."

The casualness of Alice Hubbard's comment caught Julie's interest. "He's a detective, Mrs. Hubbard!" she exclaimed.

"And a detective is a detective."

"I don't understand."

"A detective isn't a popular person. Especially not here—and certainly not now, with all that's been happening."

"We warned him about going to the Holderman Ranch," said Julie. "Both Mother and I advised against it." She stopped abruptly. "What you meant before is that I—I didn't regard Mr. Corbett as a—a person, I guess. Just a detective." She frowned. "From the little I've seen of Mr. Corbett, I—I admire him a great deal. I guess I've put that badly."

"No, you've made it quite clear. You couldn't possibly regard him as, well, in the same way, as Barney McCorkle."

Julie was startled. Her face flushed and she exhibited marked confusion. "That's ridiculous!" she exclaimed. "I hardly know him. And as for Barney, I *hate* him! I don't know what I ever saw in him."

"Let's go into the house, Julie," said Mrs. Hubbard quietly. "I'll make some coffee."

Julie accompanied Mrs. Hubbard into the ranch house and

remained for twenty minutes, but she was ill at ease. Her mind was on the conversation they had had outside and it put a restraint upon her that Mrs. Hubbard could not ease. When Julie took her departure, Mrs. Hubbard said, "It's only ten o'clock. You're going back to Seven Oaks now?"

"I've got some shopping to do," declared Julie. "That's why I really came to town."

It was a lie and Julie knew it, but it was the best she could do at the moment.

In Seven Oaks Julie rode up to Brady's store. She had not really had anything in mind to buy, but she went in and found Cathy Brady sorting mail at the rear of the store. She had never really been a close friend of Cathy, but they were within a year or two of each other's age and of course had known each other from childhood. But Cathy Brady was a town girl and Julie had been raised on a ranch. However, Julie was aware that Cathy might soon be living upon a ranch, which just happened to be as near to her home as any other ranch in the valley.

Cathy looked up from her work, saw Julie and reacted with pleasure. "Hi, Julie."

"It's nice to see you again, Cathy," said Julie. "Keeping busy?"

"Reading the postcards?" Cathy laughed. "You'd never believe some of the things people write on postcards."

"You mean, you *do* read them?"

"Of course. If people don't want things read they can pay a penny extra and use envelopes." Cathy shrugged. "Something I can do for you?"

"Yes, I need some thread. Uh, number ten Belding lisle. Red—and I'll take a spool of black too."

Cathy pointed to a counter display case nearby. "Help yourself."

Julie examined the different spools of thread with more than ordinary interest. In fact she could not seem to make up her mind. Cathy, shooting a glance at her a couple of times from her mail sorting, moved over.

"Heard what happened to that detective?" she asked.

"I've seen him," replied Julie. "He's hurt pretty badly."

"You've *seen* him?" exclaimed Cathy. "I thought he was at the hotel and couldn't get out of bed . . ."

"That's where I saw him, at the hotel."

"You went to his room?" cried Cathy.

"Why not?"

Cathy shook her head in admiration. "I wish *I* had that much nerve."

"You mean you've never gone out to Tracy's place?" flashed Julie.

"Not really. I mean, not alone. One—one Sunday Dad drove out there and I went with him, but I wouldn't go there alone. I'd be afraid to."

"Are you afraid of *him?*"

"Of course not."

"Then you're afraid of what people might say?"

"Well, you know how people are. Besides," Cathy sent a quick glance at her father who was at the front of the store with a customer, "Dad would give me holy hell if I went out there alone."

"Surely he knows that you're engaged . . ."

"But we're not. Not really. If we were I guess I'd go out there if I felt like it and I wouldn't care what people said." She hesitated. "You know what Mrs. Hubbard said yesterday? She thought that maybe Tracy ought to be called the *slow* Holderman."

"The *scared* Holderman would be more like it," said Julie brashly. "People been waiting for you two to set the date for ages and ages, and the suspense is getting to be too much. Why don't you *make* him propose?"

A light frown had come over Cathy's face. Her mouth tightened and a gleam came into her eyes. "I threw a few little digs at him yesterday and he didn't like it one bit. He's coming to town again this afternoon and I think I'll give it to him a little stronger." She shook her head. "You know that detective, he tried to make a date with me the first day he was in town. If Tracy had some of his spunk—" she stopped, noting the peculiar look on Julie's face. "I say, something wrong?"

"No, no, Cathy. Go ahead."

"I guess that's about it." Cathy sighed. Then she became alert. "Oh-oh!"

Julie had heard the opening of the door and, turning, saw that Eben Smith, the deputy sheriff, had entered the store. She had never exchanged a word with him, but she knew the man by sight. And now Eben Smith came along the length of the store, walking deliberately, purposefully.

His destination was quite obviously Julie and when he came up he nodded carelessly. "You're the Forest girl."

"My name is Julie Forest," replied Julie coolly.

"I got somethin' to say to you about that detective you hired . . ."

There was a nastiness in the deputy's tone that stiffened

Julie even more than her natural antipathy to the man. She said abruptly, "I don't believe I'd be interested in anything *you'd* have to say to me."

Eben Smith bared his teeth. "Don't try that high and mighty stuff on me. I'm going to talk to you and you're going to listen . . ."

"I can't stop you from talking," said Julie, "but I don't have to listen." She turned her back abruptly on the deputy.

Eben Smith started to reach for her, thought better of it, then stepped around her so that he again faced her. "It's for his own good—and yours, Miss Uppity. You tell that blasted detective that I warned him the other night to mind his p's and q's around here and if he goes stirrin' up people I'm going to run him out of the county."

"Are you through?" asked Julie angrily.

"I've said what I come to say. You tell him."

"Tell him yourself."

"You're the one's runnin' in an' out to him," snapped Eben Smith. "Visitin' him at the hotel in broad daylight . . ."

Julie's hand flashed up and slapped the deputy in the face.

Eben Smith let out a roar of rage and lunged for Julie. He caught her arm as she tried to escape from him, and whirled her around.

"You little hussy," he snarled, "I'm gonna give you the goddamdest lickin' you ever had. Somethin' your paw shoulda done . . ."

Julie struggled furiously to get out of his grip, and her struggle enabled her to take only glancingly the open-handed blow that Smith lashed out at her. He was trying to hit her a second time when Jeff Brady came rushing down behind the long counter. He caught up a shotgun from below the counter and leveled it at the deputy. "Smith!" he cried. "If you hit her again I'll blow your head off!"

Smith reacted as if struck with a club. He was frozen for an instant, then released Julie.

"No damn woman's gonna slap me," he snarled.

"And no man's going to hit a woman in my presence," retorted Jeff Brady. "Now clear out of here—and don't ever come back in here. I mean that, Smith!"

"You talk big because you think your brother's payin' me my salary . . ."

"Link isn't paying you, the people of this county are," said Jeff Brady angrily. "And I know damn well Link isn't going to like what happened here when he hears about it."

"Go ahead, blab to him," sneered Eben Smith. He gave Julie a look of venomous contempt, spared some of it on Jeff

59

Brady, then made the long walk to the door, his boots clumping heavily, spitefully. He went out of the store.

"Thank you, Mr. Brady," Julie said then.

"It's all right, Julie," said Jeff Brady. "That man's more outlaw than lawman. I warned Link when he first asked about hiring him. But he thought he needed a man who could face the gun fighters that've been brought in on their own level. I'm sorry, I didn't mean that as a slap to your father."

"I know, Mr. Brady. Father always spoke well of you—and the sheriff too." A shudder ran through her. "That man makes my skin crawl. He's a killer, the kind—" she stopped, thinking of her father. She drew in a deep breath. "Thank you again, Mr. Brady."

Then, forgetting the spools of thread she had put aside, she went out of the store. When the door closed, Cathy said to her father, "That girl's got more spunk than I'd have in a million years."

"I like her," said Jeff Brady. He laid the shotgun on the counter, then held out his right arm. It was trembling violently. Cathy noted it and said, "Would you really have shot him, Dad?"

"I couldn't have," said Jeff Brady. "The gun ain't loaded!"

On the street, Julie walked swiftly to the hotel, but the scene in the general store had left its mark on her. She was actually trembling when she entered the hotel and, instead of heading for the stairs, she whirled on Gregson who was watching her from behind the desk.

"Mr. Gregson," she said, "would you make sure that some food is sent up to Mr. Corbett? And tell him that I—I couldn't come back, but I'll be here this evening to check on him."

"I'll send up a tray right-away," said Gregson.

"Thank you."

Julie went out, got on her horse and galloped it most of the way back to the Forest Ranch.

Chapter Twelve

The tray had been brought to Corbett's room, but he did not eat any of the food. He was awake, his eyes studying the fly-spotted ceiling, when there was a firm knock on the door. It was shortly after two o'clock.

"Yes?" he called.

There was no reply, but the knock was repeated. "All right, all right," he called irritably. "The door's open. Come in!"

The door was opened and Corbett, turning painfully, saw Alice Hubbard standing in the doorway. A groan was torn from his lips. She closed the door and came forward.

"I heard you'd been hurt," she said. Then she added quickly, "But that isn't why I came. I also heard that you were a detective and since I am greatly interested in stopping cattle rustling, I thought I should cooperate with you."

"The Forest family's paying me to find the man who killed Sam Forest," said Corbett. "Nobody's hired me to stop cattle rustling."

"I think you'll find the two things tie in together," said Alice Hubbard. "I thought you might be interested to know what I've done so far . . ."

"You sent a telegram to the Secretary of the Interior," said Corbett.

She stared down at him. "You know that!"

"I also know that you've hired fourteen gunhands in the last six months and you haven't fired any help during that same period." He made a very small gesture with his hand, which sent pain lancing up to his shoulder. "That information cost me two hundred dollars—in bribes." His eyes met hers clearly for the first time since she had come into the room. "A detective'll stoop to anything."

"You're consistent," said Alice Hubbard. "You ran yourself down the other day and you're doing it again."

"The first lesson a detective gets is how to lie. It's also the second and third lesson."

"All right," said Alice Hubbard, "there's nothing I can tell you . . ."

"You'll excuse me for not getting up, ma'am?"

She nodded and started to go when Corbett said, "That's the best way to stop rustling. Eliminate the market for stolen beef and remove the profit in rustling."

She turned back, regarding him thoughtfully for a moment. "The cattle are going through the badlands," she said, "that's obvious. But where are the cattle going on the other side? North, there's nothing but desert. West, south there are the Indian reservations. And Fort Miller two hundred miles away. Not too far."

"You think the Indian agents are in with the outlaws?"

"They have to be," said Mrs. Hubbard. "I didn't want to put it that flatly to the secretary, but I think Governor Walters will make it stronger . . ."

"How did you get in touch with the governor—by telegraph?"

"No, I wrote him. Oh, there've been several letters back and forth."

Corbett nodded. "Don't use the telegraph."

"It's Bonner you bribed?"

"If I were you I'd use the mail," said Corbett, giving her the answer indirectly.

She left then. There was no verbal goodbye, no slightest sign of surrender in her coolness. A bare nod, then she was out of the room, closing the door carefully behind her.

Corbett remained perfectly still for five minutes after Alice Hubbard had gone. Then he drew a slow, deep breath and making a tremendous effort, sat upon the bed. A gasp was torn from him, but he persisted and swung his feet to the floor. Then he began to exercise. He moved his head from side to side, rolled it about in a circular motion and even opened and closed his mouth. He repeated each movement over and over. In two minutes perspiration had broken out on his face.

He clenched his hands, opening and closing them slowly, then faster, putting on more pressure. He worked upward, began moving his arms back and forth and finally, when the perspiration was streaming down his face, began moving his upper torso from side to side, then turning his body back and forth. It was twenty minutes before he finally stood up on his feet and began moving his legs.

He spent a solid hour on the dreadful exercise, clenching his teeth and, at times, his fists. Only his will power kept him at it and when he finished with one part of his body, he returned to another.

He moved back and forth across the narrow confines of his room to the window, to the door. He sat down, got up. And, finally, as a last test of his endurance, he peeled off his shirt and, standing before the cracked mirror over the washstand, shaved himself carefully, deliberately, working over and around the bruises. He wound up by taking off his Levis and donning the spare ones he still had in his blanket roll.

He wanted more than anything else in the world to drop back on the bed and rest, rest for a day or two, but he forced himself to open the door, walk out and down the stairs.

Gregson was behind the desk and stared open-mouthed when he saw Corbett. "Hey, you ain't hurt so bad after all!"

"All I needed was a little rest," said Corbett. He crossed the lobby, opened the door and stepped out to the sidewalk. He stood in front of the hotel a moment or two, then started left, toward the saloon, then past it to Brady's General Store.

He entered. Cathy was in the post office section, talking to a customer, but Brady, in front, was straightening up some stock. He stared at Corbett in astonishment.

"I want to buy a revolver," Corbett said to Brady.

Brady blinked, then came quickly forward. "Of course. Frontier Model?"

He brought one out from a display. Corbett took the gun, tried the hammer, then let the hammer down carefully by pulling the trigger, but keeping his thumb on the hammer. "Little stiff," he observed.

"Needs oil, that's all."

"How much is it?"

"Twenty dollars."

"How about a Winchester? A forty-five, seventy-five?"

"Just happen to have one."

The rifle was on a wall display, but Brady took it down. Corbett sized up the gun, tried the lever a time or two, then said, "I'll take them both. Charge them up to Pete Holderman."

"What?"

"The old man," said Corbett.

"Well, now," said Brady, "I don't think I can do that."

"Why not?"

Brady hesitated. "Well, I heard what happened out there and I know Pete isn't going to pay for these guns."

"He's got my Winchester and Colt," said Corbett. "It's a fair exchange."

Cathy, who had been listening to the interchange between her father and Corbett, left her post office booth and came along behind the counter.

"Let him have them, Dad."

"It's fifty-seven dollars and fifty cents," said Jeff Brady. "You know how hard it is to get money out of Pete Holder-

63

man anyway. And in view of what's happened he isn't going to pay *this* bill."

"He'll pay it," said Corbett earnestly, "I promise you that."

Brady shook his head. "I don't want to get caught in the middle of a fight between you and the Holdermans. I already had trouble today because of you . . ."

"Who with?" asked Corbett.

Brady winced. "It's all right. I'm sorry I mentioned it."

"Who'd you have the trouble with?" persisted Corbett.

Brady was still not inclined to tell, but Cathy Brady burst out, "Eben Smith. He came in here when Julie Forest was here and said some nasty things to her about you—and her. She slapped his face and then he hit her."

"Be damned," exclaimed Corbett.

"That isn't all," continued Cathy. "Dad threw down on the deputy with a shotgun and made him leave the store. Told him never to come back." Then she added, for dessert, "The shotgun was empty."

Corbett stared at the discomfited storekeeper. He exhaled heavily. "Fifty-seven, fifty, you said?"

He took money from his pocket and counted out the exact amount. Then he slipped the empty Colt into the holster he was wearing and thrust the Winchester under his left arm.

Cathy Brady said, "You're a pretty tough *hombre*, aren't you, Mr. Corbett?"

"Right now," said Corbett, "I'm about as tough as soft milk toast."

He walked stiffly out of the store.

He barely made it back to the hotel and had to grit his teeth as he climbed the stairs. Inside he leaned the rifle against the wall, then stepped to the bed and collapsed upon it.

Chapter Thirteen

Julie Forest was peeling potatoes when her mother came into the kitchen. She had been taking a nap when Julie had arrived home, and Julie had not wanted to disturb her. Actually she had been in her bedroom lying on the bed. But she had not been sleeping. She had been thinking—of the years of her life, the long years she had been married. Sam had been difficult at times and there had been many quarrels between them, but thinking about it now, Helen Forest knew that she would not have wanted it any different. Nor would have Sam. He had not lived a quiet life himself and he was not a calm man by nature and he would not have wanted a placid wife or, for that matter, a passive daughter.

He had not had them.

Mrs. Forest watched Julie a moment or two, then she said, "How is he?"

Julie flashed a look at her mother over her shoulder. "He's been badly hurt, but not seriously. I—I took him up his breakfast and made him eat." She hesitated. "Do you think I shouldn't have gone to his room?"

"Julie," said her mother, "you're old enough to make up your own mind about such things." Then, "Do *you* think you did wrong?"

"No, Mother, I don't," replied Julie. "Only—there might be some talk about it. That deputy sheriff heard about it and said some nasty things to me about it. I slapped his face."

Mrs. Forest exclaimed, "Where was this—in the hotel?"

"No, at Brady's store later. He hit me and then Mr. Brady threatened to shoot him with a shotgun. The story's probably all over town by now."

Mrs. Forest seated herself on the nearest chair. "Well, you've had a day of it!"

"I'm going back to town this evening. He can't move from his room and he'll have to eat."

"You took him his food at breakfast and dinner?"

"No, just breakfast. I—I asked Mr. Gregson to see that he received it at noon."

65

"Perhaps it would be best to ask Mr. Gregson again this evening."

A frown creased Julie's smooth forehead. "I'd still have to ride into town and tell him."

"We could go together in the buckboard," suggested Mrs. Forest. "I need the air and the exercise."

Julie turned back to her work, but a moment later she said, "I went out and visited with Mrs. Hubbard. I like her. She must have been a beautiful woman at one time. She still is, for that matter."

"I thought her the most striking woman I had ever seen when she and her husband first settled here. Let's see, that was sixteen, eighteen, no, sixteen years ago."

"Strange they never had any children."

Mrs. Forest hesitated a moment, then she said, "Mrs. Hubbard is a very reserved woman, but we used to visit back and forth in the early days. She'd been married once before. She told me that, but I don't think it's generally known. She was raised on a hard-scrabble farm in southwest Texas and she and her first husband were dirt farmers. From things she let drop, they did not have any easy time of it and her husband died when their only child was only four or five years old. Then she married Mr. Hubbard and after awhile they deserted the farm and came west. They liked it here and settled down, but instead of farming they went in for cattle raising."

"What happened to the child? Did it die?"

"N-no. That was the one subject that Alice was touchy about. I got the feeling that there was some difficulty with Tom Hubbard about the child and, well, I really don't know *exactly* what happened. I think the boy disappeared at a very early age, ran away from home. Or perhaps her first husband's family took him. I don't think it was that, however—" she stopped, looked at Julie's face. There was a peculiar look in her daughter's eyes. "What is it?"

"While you were talking," Julie said, "I had the strangest feeling about—about Mrs. Hubbard and her son." She suddenly shook her head. "No, it's just one of those wild ideas that I get once in awhile."

"What is it?"

"You'll laugh at me."

"You've gone this far, you might as well go through with it."

"Today—when I looked down at him, in his room, his face was all battered and bruised. But it was still a strong face and I thought of another strong face I knew. I thought of it again, when I was with Mrs. Hubbard . . ."

Mrs. Forest was silent so long that Julie finally turned to

66

look at her mother. Helen Forest nodded quietly, thoughtfully.

"Yesterday, when they were both here, although not at the same time, I had an uneasy feeling about them—about Alice, rather. She reminded me of someone I had seen not long before. I couldn't put a finger on it at the time, but now—now I can see the resemblance." She shook her head, sighed. "It's ridiculous, they *couldn't* be related!"

"Mother, how old would you say Mrs. Hubbard was? She doesn't look more than about forty-five."

"Oh, she's considerably more than that. Probably fifty-two or three. Let's see, she told me once how old she was. She said she was a year older than I was and I'm fifty-one now. Yes, that would make her fifty-two."

"Then she couldn't possibly be his mother, could she? Mr. Corbett's in his late thirties."

"He may not be that old. Doing the kind of work he does, he'd age early. Although we know so little about him really. We have no idea how long he's been a detective; what, if anything, he did before he became a detective."

"He won't talk about himself. Do you know I know absolutely nothing about him? Nothing, except that he's a detective."

It was dark in Corbett's room when he awakened. For a moment he lay still, listening to the noises of the street. Apparently the evening's activities had begun. It took him a moment to gather his thoughts, but then he sat up suddenly, swinging his legs to the floor.

A spasm of pain shot through him and for a moment he thought he would fall back on the bed, but then he steeled himself and began swinging his arms back and forth. He got to his feet, staggered, then regained full possession of his muscles. Clenching his teeth, he performed a quick set of exercises. He was still at it when there was a knock at the door.

Corbett stepped to the door, pulled it open. The hallway was lighted and he saw Gregson with a tray of food in his hands. "She was back with her mother. Said to bring this up to you and tell you to be sure and eat."

Corbett gestured to the chair. "Put it there."

Gregson set down the tray and tried to peer into Corbett's face in the semidarkness. "You feel better?"

"Well enough. Thank you, Mr. Gregson."

Gegson backed out of the room, but he left the door ajar. Corbett closed it, then struck a match and applied it to the lamp. When the room sprang into light he went to his blanket roll and rummaged for a box of .45-.75 rifle cartridges. He filled the Winchester, then took .45 shells from his holster and loaded the Frontier Model. He tried it in the holster, found that it was smooth enough. He remembered, however, that the weapon itself was stiff and made a mental note of that.

He then gathered together all of his belongings, packed them securely in the blanket roll and, picking it up together with the rifle, he left his room.

He walked heavily down to the lobby. The night clerk was on duty at the desk, Gregson nowhere in sight. The man noted the rifle and blanket roll.

"Checking out, Mr. Corbett?" he asked.

"No, I'll be back."

"Tonight?"

Corbett shrugged and headed for the door. The clerk called after him, "I think you ought to pay your rent if you're going to be gone awhile."

"I said I'd be back," snapped Corbett and went out.

On the street he crossed to the livery stable. He found his horse in a stall munching hay. He found his saddle nearby, put it on the animal, then threw on the blanket roll and lashed it down. He was putting the rifle into the scabbard when the liveryman came out of his little room at the rear.

"Leavin'?"

"How much do I owe you?" countered Corbett.

"Two dollars ought to do it," said the liveryman. "I took real good care of your horse. He's a fine animal and . . ."

Corbett walked out of the stall, leaving his horse tied to the manger. "I'll be back for him later."

Leaving the livery stable, he crossed the street diagonally, reaching the sidewalk in front of the saloon. He stepped up to the batwing doors, stopped and peered over the top.

His eyes darted quickly about the room and focused upon a card table halfway down the right side of the room. Bonner was at the table; Jeff Brady was not, but Eben Smith was there scanning a poker hand.

Corbett pushed open the batwing door with his left hand. With his right he drew his Frontier Model. He let it hang from his hand, the muzzle pointing at the floor as he walked into the saloon. He had gone a dozen feet before a sudden hush fell upon the room.

Eben Smith, cards in one hand, money in the other looked up—at the Frontier Model that Corbett whipped up. Corbett was then only ten feet away, but the table was between him and Smith.

"On your feet, Smith," said Corbett.

"You gone crazy?" gasped Smith.

"Up," said Corbett, "or take it sitting down."

Eben Smith let the money and cards fall from his hands. But he still made no move to get up. "You know what you're doing? I could beat you with your head start."

"Try it!" invited Corbett. He started carefully around the table. Smith moved his chair to face Corbett when he came around. But he still did not make his play. His eyes were locked with Corbett's—or, rather, one of them, for his right eye was almost closed from swelling. And even the other seemed only half-opened.

Then, when Corbett stopped only a yard or two from him, Eben Smith slowly began to rise. "We can finish this outside," he said thickly.

"You're not getting an even break from me," said Corbett, his voice deadly low, but ringing. "I'm not playing your game."

Smith had reached his feet and his hands moved up slowly, carefully past his waist to show Corbett, and the spectators that he was not going for his gun. Not unless Corbett could be distracted for an instant.

"If you're not going to draw," said Corbett, "I'm going to teach you a lesson that you'll remember as long as you live."

"Because of that piece of fluff?" cried Eben Smith. "She's nothing but a . . ."

Corbett struck him with the gun. It was a backhand, raking blow so that the barrel smashed against Eben Smith's face and the sight ripped his nose and cheekbone. Blood spurted instantly from the wound and Smith cried out in pain. His right hand darted down then. He was going for his gun.

But Corbett brought back the gun from the end of its pendulum swing and this time he put more weight behind it. The barrel of the gun cracked against Smith's jaw with a smack that could be heard in every corner of the saloon.

Smith went down like an axed steer. He hit the floor, unconscious.

Corbett stepped quickly backward and turned sideward. His eyes went around the faces that were watching as if hypnotized.

"Anybody want to take it up?" he asked ringingly.

He waited a count of three and when there was no response from anyone in the room, walked stiffly out of the saloon, the .45 still in his hand.

Outside he holstered the Frontier Model and recrossed to the livery stable. He entered, got his horse out of the stall and mounted it. He rode out of the stable, passing the liveryman just inside the door.

On the street he turned left. A man was just coming out of

the sheriff's office. It was Link Brady. Corbett turned his horse toward Brady.

"You're leaving?" asked the sheriff.

Corbett made a gesture that was no answer at all. He said, "I just pistol-whipped your deputy. He's over at the saloon." His right hand hung loosely at his side, a fact of which Brady took note.

The sheriff said, "Serves the sonofabitch right. I heard what happened at Jeff's place this afternoon. Eben had it coming. Is he dead?"

"I don't think so, but even if he is, I'm riding out."

"You coming back?"

"I don't know," said Corbett and kneed his horse. He rode past the sheriff, kicked his horse gently and it went into a swift trot.

Chapter Fourteen

In the early evening the sky had been overcast and Corbett followed the road in almost total darkness, his sure-footed horse traveling without difficulty. He passed the Forest Ranch and had trouble finding the turn-off to the tiny ranch of the good Holderman, but once on the trail Corbett soon left it.

He passed Tracy's log cabin at a distance, recognizing the landmark only because he caught a glimmer of light off to the right.

He rode on, the land getting rougher as he began climbing. He rode through clumps of cattle, but he was on the land of the real Holdermans and he pressed on continuously.

The clouds became patchier after awhile and the stars were bright, so that he could see well enough at times. That worried Corbett more than the total darkness, for the Holdermans surely had night riders on the range and one thing Corbett most decidedly did not want was to be seen by one of them. He felt well enough as long as he remained in the saddle, but he knew that once he dismounted he would be as stiff as he had been earlier in the day.

Yet he could not ride through the night. He was on unfamiliar terrain, he could not scout the country ahead and for all he knew he was headed in the wrong direction.

He gave it up shortly after eleven o'clock. He found himself in a narrow coulee, with an almost sheer cliff on his left and a scrubby patch of trees on the right. The sky had cleared and, with the moon now shining and the stars flickering, it was almost light enough to read a newspaper.

He stopped his horse at the edge of a patch of trees, dismounted with vast difficulty, then tethered his horse to a tree. He took down the blanket roll, but left the animal saddled, although he did loosen the cinch a notch or two.

He put the lariat on the horse then, tying one end to a tree so that the horse could graze within a limited range.

71

By the time he had completed his chores, Corbett did not feel like unrolling his blanket roll and used it as a pillow instead. He closed his eyes and was asleep within two minutes.

The whickering of his horse awakened Corbett. For a moment he lay still, listening to the sounds of the night, then he got to his feet and, moving as quickly as he could to his horse, put one hand on the animal's nostrils. It was well that he did, for he soon heard the ringing of metal on rock. A horse was going by not too far from where he stood.

Keeping perfectly still, he saw the horse a moment later. It was plodding heavily along, ridden by a man hunched over in the saddle whom Corbett could not of course recognize. He waited a good five minutes before taking his hand off his horse's nose.

Taking out his watch, he peered at it. He had slept five hours. It was after four o'clock in the morning. The dawn would soon be breaking.

He picked up his blanket roll, strapped it onto his horse, then, while tightening the saddle cinch, suddenly realized that he was doing his work and moving about with considerably less effort and pain than the evening before.

In another day he would be even better and in two or three days—Corbett shrugged. He might be willing to try the Holdermans again, but under his own conditions. The same kind of conditions he had used against Eben Smith, gun fighter-deputy sheriff.

Although he was ready for traveling, Corbett remained where he was for another ten minutes, holding the reins in one hand and permitting his horse to continue grazing. Finally he slapped him lightly on the flank and mounted.

He rode easily, allowing his mount to pick its way through the coulee. The ground was rough, sloping upward as he rode along. He reached the top of a ridge in fifteen or twenty minutes, then stopping, turned in the saddle and saw that the false dawn was lighting up the sky in the east.

He sat his horse a few minutes, then kneeing it, continued on, although now he was riding downhill. The light dimmed for a few minutes, but then the real dawn began to unfold itself and he was able to see his surroundings. The first thing he noted were a half-dozen scattered steers. He wondered if they wandered here from the Holderman Ranch, or whether they were rustled animals that had strayed. There was little enough grazing here for them, but there was water, Corbett saw, a winding, shallow stream that came from the higher ground on the left.

Corbett rode through the valley and began climbing the

slope beyond. It was steeper than the one he had ascended in the darkness, but not steep enough to interfere with his riding. He watched the rocky ground on both sides of his path and several times when the rockiness was not as apparent, he saw signs of heavy traffic of cloven hoofs. This was the route for the rustlers, all right.

It was midmorning when he reached the crest and he was beginning to think of food. He was used to going for long periods without food, but in his weakened condition he seemed to want something to build up his strength.

He had become careless as he neared the top, for suddenly a man stepped out from behind a boulder. He had a Winchester rifle in his hand, but it was not pointed at Corbett. In fact the man, although he was obviously a guard or lookout, did not seem too concerned about Corbett.

He gave a careless wave of his free hand.

"Hi, pardner," he greeted Corbett.

Corbett pulled up. "Anybody down in the valley?" he asked.

The lookout shrugged. "Probably. Depends on what you got in your pocket."

"Such as what?"

"Money or hardware."

"What kind of hardware?"

"Stars, badges." The man became a bit more alert. "If you're a lawman, this is your last chance to turn back—and I don't think you'll make it back because you passed Burt Rackin a mile or so back."

Corbett exclaimed in chagrin. "I passed a man and didn't see him?"

"Burt's kinda hard to see when he don't want to be seen."

"You going to try to stop me?" asked Corbett.

"Uh-uh. You don't look like a lawman to me, but if you are, well, that's too bad. For you." The lookout grinned. "But I was you I still wouldn't go ahead if I didn't have the right kind of passport."

"Passport?"

"Money."

"This is a toll road?"

"When I was a tadpole," said the lookout, "my paw told me there wasn't nothin' free in this world. That was a long time ago, but I never did get nothin' for nothin' and it ain't no different here. You pay your way."

He took a sideward step, made a sweeping gesture for Corbett. "Long's you know the rules . . ."

Corbett shook his head dubiously and rode past the man. He wondered for a moment if a bullet would hit him in the

73

back, but the man had obviously had the drop on him and if he hadn't done anything before, he would not do so now.

Corbett rode down into a wooded valley, in which there were signs of habitation, a tree stump recently made with an ax, branches from a trimmed trunk, a grazing horse and soon, the best indication of all, woodsmoke. He smelled it first, but soon saw it.

The well-traveled trail made a right turn and Corbett rode into a small clearing. A log cabin stood at the far edge of it and not far from it were two or three lean-tos. Smoke came from the cabin as well as from a couple of outdoor fires near the lean-tos.

There were horses in the clearing, and men.

Corbett saw only two or three at first but, as he neared the tiny settlement, he saw that there were at least a half-dozen around the lean-tos and another one coming out of the cabin. He saw Corbett approaching and stood waiting for him to ride up.

Corbett was seen by others and two or three left their fires and went in the direction of the cabin toward which Corbett was headed.

As he neared the group, Corbett became aware that there wasn't an unarmed man in the group. They were a ragged, unkempt-looking crowd. Only the man before the cabin was clean-shaven. The others were whiskered, their clothes were dirty, sometimes trousers and shirts were patched, more often they were simply ripped and torn and left that way.

The clean-shaven man, who was obviously a leader, signaled to Corbett to dismount. "Light," he said.

Corbett prepared himself for the ordeal, determined to climb down without revealing any indications of bodily injury. There was no use letting these men know that he was not in the most perfect of physical conditions. The damage to his face he could not help, but that wasn't important.

He swung lightly from the saddle, landing heavily and for a moment almost stumbling, but he recovered himself. He sniffed visibly and audibly.

"I could use some of that beefsteak," he said.

"You got a handle?" demanded the shaven man.

"Any special name you prefer? Smith, Jones . . . ?"

"That ain't goin' to get you anything but a hard time," snapped the man before Corbett.

"All right, the name's Corbett. What's yours?"

"Boggs," was the reply. "It ain't the name I was born with, but I been usin' it quite a spell and it's simple, easy to remember and I can spell it. Who licked you?"

"Nobody," said Corbett. "I had a tussle a couple, three days ago, but I didn't get licked or I wouldn't be here."

"Where was that, Seven Oaks?"

"That's the town back a-ways where they got a sheriff and a courthouse? Uh-uh, it was back a piece. I didn't stop at Seven Oaks. Town that size usually has a pretty strong jail. The one I was in wasn't more'n a shack and all I had to do was take away the marshal's gun. That's how I got the scratches."

"You talk good," observed Boggs. "Maybe too good. You just passin' through here?"

"Depends," said Corbett. "I could use a couple of days' rest, but some of these small town marshals they're like 'Paches, they don't never quit."

"Won't no marshal bother you here," said Boggs. "Not no live marshal. That's if you got the price."

"Price? What price?"

"Well, let's see what you're carryin'. Empty your pockets and we'll take a look."

Corbett brought up his right hand carelessly and hooked his thumb on the cartridge belt. "I'll pay for a square meal," he said, "if the price ain't too high."

"I said empty."

Corbett said, "I've got a little money. I don't mind paying my way."

"Mister," said Boggs, "I told you to empty your pockets. I've told you twice and I ain't going to tell you a third time . . ."

He took a step forward.

With his left hand Corbett suddenly reached into the pocket of his Levis. He brought out a thick sheaf of money.

"I said I'd pay my way. Now what do you consider a fair price?"

One of the men nearest Corbett moved forward and peered at the money in Corbett's hand. "If they're all twenties," he said to Boggs, "he's got a fine wad."

"Three hundred dollars," said Corbett. "Maybe a few dollars more."

Boggs grunted, surprised. "That much? Most of the fellas comin' here been runnin' so hard they usually don't have much with 'em. Tell you what, a hundred dollars'll keep you here a week . . ."

The man who had estimated Corbett's money suddenly exclaimed. "That's a brand new six-gun he's wearin'!"

Corbett made a quick gesture with his thumb toward the Winchester in the saddle scabbard. "So's the rifle. This place I had the ruckus, there was a store there and the marshal not

75

bein' able to make his rounds, I thought I might as well get me a couple new pieces of hardware." He grunted. "Imagine my surprise when I found this money in the till. I ain't usually this well-heeled."

Boggs shook his head in admiration. "That was thinkin' real good. I like a man thinks good." He held out his hand.

Corbett moved up and counted out five twenty-dollar gold certificates into the waiting palm of Boggs' hand. Boggs nodded in satisfaction.

"We kinda share and share alike around here. I've had my breakfast, but any the boys still cookin', just set with them and feed yourself. I'll talk to you later."

Corbett made a tour of the lean-tos. At one there was a fire, but nothing was cooking; at the second the men had already eaten, but at the third he found a grizzled outlaw of sixty-odd holding a chunk of beef, impaled on a ramrod, over the fire.

"That smells good," said Corbett.

"Tastes good too. Yearling. I butchered her myself," replied the oldster. Then he chuckled wickedly. "A stray."

"From the Holderman Ranch?" asked Corbett. "Or the Forest?"

"Who looks at the brand?" asked the old outlaw. He withdrew the meat from the fire, and, laying it on a tin plate, pulled out the ramrod. "This is the way we used to cook when I was with Sherman in Georgia."

"On the march to the sea?" exclaimed Corbett. "What regiment?"

"Twenty-fourth Illinois."

"A good outfit."

The grizzled outlaw pointed at Corbett. "Hell, that was fifteen years ago. *You* wasn't old enough . . ."

"I was nineteen," said Corbett. "I was seventeen at Vicksburg—and I'd been in the Army a year. Fourth Missouri Cavalry."

"That was a Dutch outfit, wasn't it?"

"The men were from eastern Missouri, a lot of them from St. Louis. But how many Dutch soldiers were there with Sherman?"

"Hell, half, I guess. Some of the goddamn colonels couldn't even talk English."

"They were good soldiers," said Corbett. "Some of them had been officers in Prussia and came over after the '48 revolution. Let's try this yearling beef . . ."

They attacked the food and Corbett ate with relish. The oldster, in between mouthfuls of beef, talked about the campaigns with Sherman, but Corbett, listening, developed the

76

idea that the man had not actually been a soldier at all. He knew the regiments, but from one or two things he dropped, Corbett became convinced that he had actually been one of the famous "bummers," that horde of camp followers that had attached itself to Sherman's army and created so much havoc with their foraging along the line of the march to the sea that Sherman, before the conclusion of his campaign, had felt forced to drive the bummers away from his army.

He did not mention this to the old man, however, but thanked him for the food and wandered off. He found a poker game going on on the open ground, the players seated cross-legged around a blanket, but the sun was shining brightly now and he stretched himself out on the ground, face uncovered.

After awhile he fell asleep.

Chapter Fifteen

Corbett slept for an hour, while the poker game went on less than a dozen feet from where he lay. He felt considerably refreshed when he awakened from sleeping in the warm sun and, sitting up, watched the card players awhile.

Finally he got to his feet and walked over to the game. "What're you playing, fellas, poker?" he asked innocently.

One of the players exclaimed, "What're we playin', fellas, poker?" he repeated mockingly. "Another cardsharp!"

"Oh, you got one here already?"

A man of about forty-five, who wore a battered green derby, grinned up at Corbett. "That's me. I used to play three-card monte on the New York Central. Never had no luck on any other train, just the New York Central, that all the city slickers rode. But they were hard losers. I cut one of 'em a little and they didn't like it at all. They were going to hang me only my pa bribed one of them Tammany politicians in New York ten thousand dollars and they let me escape."

"It's ten thousand now," exclaimed one of the other players. "It used to be only five."

"That's right," said another man, "and the reward for you went up too. How much is it now?"

"Five thousand," chuckled the monte man.

"For five thousand Eben Smith'd come in here and take you," chortled another player.

"Eben Smith," said Corbett. "I've heard that name. Bad medicine, isn't he?"

"Bad enough," said the man who had mentioned his name. "Especially since he's wearin' a tin star."

"Come on, come on," cried one of the men impatiently. "We gonna play poker or we gonna gab all day?"

"Mind if I sit in a hand or two?" asked Corbett.

"Your money's as good as anyone else's," was the reply from one of the men, "unless you printed it yourself." He looked up suspiciously. "Did you?"

Corbett grinned and sat down cross-legged on the edge of the blanket. There were six other men around the blanket and the amount of money before each man was surprisingly large. Some of them had greenbacks and silver, plus a few gold pieces, but the three-card monte man seemed to have only gold, which he kept in a leather pouch before him. It was more than half-filled.

It was three-card monte man's deal. "This is five card stud," he announced.

"What's the limit?" asked Corbett.

"What you got in your pocket," was the reply.

Corbett let out a low whistle. The dealer dealt one card swiftly all around, down, then the second card up. Corbett had a ten up. He bent over and peered at his hole card. It was a jack of hearts, which matched the ten. The cards were grimy, worn from much usage. In a town they would have been discarded long ago.

"Ace bets," announced the dealer.

"I got 'em backed up," said the man with the ace up. "Gonna cost you twenty dollars."

Nobody believed him and nobody commented on the size of the bet. Two men called the bet, then it was up to Corbett. He tossed in a twenty-dollar bill. "I'll see one more card."

The others also called and the three-card monte man dealt the second card up. Corbett's card was the queen of hearts. The man on his left had paired up eights, neither of them the heart, however.

"Eights bet," said the dealer.

"I'll suck you boys in," said the man with the pair of eights. "Twenty."

One man dropped out. The others all called. Corbett's third card up was the king of hearts. He had a four-card potential straight flush. The dealer dealt himself a second seven and the man on his right got the ace of hearts, giving him a pair.

"Aces bet!"

One of the players swore roundly and threw in his cards. The man with the aces counted out fifty dollars. "Got to protect the winning hand." The next man promptly turned down his cards. Corbett put in his fifty dollars quietly and the man with the eights put it in with poor grace.

"Just enough to make me have to see the last card."

The dealer with his pair of sevens tossed in three twenty-dollar gold pieces, took out an eagle in change. "Last card coming up."

He dealt slowly, giving the man with the aces a queen. He made a flourish and turned up the trey of hearts for Corbett. "And a busted straight."

"Could still be a flush," said the man on Corbett's left.

"He didn't bet it like that," said the dealer. He tossed the man a third eight, then gave himself his second inconsequential pair.

"Three eights bet!"

The man with the three eights was very unhappy about having the top hand showing. "With my luck, I know I'll walk into it. I check."

"Mister Chicken checks," announced the dealer.

"Me, too," growled the man with the aces.

Corbett counted all the money he had before him, which was actually all that he had. One hundred and thirty-four dollars. He shoved it into the center of the blanket.

"The works."

The man with the three eights let out a roar. "A flush!"

"Call it and see," said Corbett quietly.

"I've got to," complained the three-eights man. He was still counting out the money when the three-card monte man leaned far across the blanket to study the cards in front of Corbett.

"If you had a possible straight flush, why didn't you bet it?"

He drew back, scowled, then turned down his hand. The man with the aces showing snapped, "Aces up, and two hands beat me."

"Flush," said Corbett and turned up his.

"Dammit," roared the man with the three eights. "He *did* have a possible straight flush—possible royal flush." He gave Corbett a look of disgust. "With that hand I'd have bet my shirt."

"Against what?"

The next man gathered up the cards. "Straight poker for a change," he said as he shuffled.

Corbett meanwhile raked in the pot, counting his money. He had over five hundred dollars.

The ante for straight poker was ten dollars, which Corbett contributed, but receiving nothing worthwhile he dropped out. It was during his wait that his eyes fell down upon the cards and he picked up his discard. He touched the edges of the cards, found them rough.

The cards were nicked with a fingernail. Not all of them. Just the face cards, perhaps the ace, which, however, Corbett could not see at the moment, having no aces.

The next hand was also straight poker and Corbett, although he had a pair of sixes, dropped out. He also had an ace which he felt carefully. It had a nick almost at the edge of the card. That was the pattern, apparently, the nick on the ace at the edge, the king nick next, then the queen and jack almost in the center of the card.

The three-card monte man won the immediate pot, raking in more than seven hundred dollars.

It was Corbett's deal. He gathered up the cards, putting them together awkwardly and, shuffling, spilled the pack. He got them together, shuffled again slowly, carefully, then put the pack out for a cut.

"Stud's been good to me," he said, "so that's what this is going to be."

The top card he saw had a nick and from the position of the nick was a jack. He dealt it. The next card was unmarked, but then he dealt a second jack and to the three-card monte man he gave an ace. The next two cards were unnicked, as was Corbett's, but it turned out to be a nine when he examined it later.

Of the turned-up cards, the three-card monte man was high with a king. He promptly opened for twenty dollars. Everyone called, including Corbett, who had a pair of nines backed up.

Corbett dealt the first man a jack, giving him a pair. The man's delight was distilled when the three-card monte man wound up with a pair of kings. The next two players received their cards, promptly turned them down. Corbett dealt himself a nine, giving him a pair up and one in the hole.

There remained only the three players, the man with the pair of jacks, the three-card monte man and Corbett with his three nines.

"The hell with it," said the man with the pair of kings and an ace in the hole. "Fifty dollars."

Corbett shook his head. "I guess I've got to pay."

The man with jacks counted out fifty with ill grace. Corbett noted from the nick that the man was going to receive a third jack.

He dealt the card and the man, although one of his jacks was concealed, let out a roar of triumph. The man with the aces frowned, but was not displeased when he received an ace, which Corbett knew gave him aces and kings.

Corbett winced a little when he saw his fourth card, an ace.

"Aces still high," he said.

"All right," said the three-card monte man, exhaling heavily, "I'll walk into it. Fifty dollars."

Corbett called and the man with three jacks studied his hole card as if he had never seen it before. Finally he shook his head. "I call and raise her fifty."

The three-card monte man exclaimed and leaning over,

peered at the man's hand, apparently recognizing the ace in the hole.

He frowned, then put in the additional fifty. Corbett called.

The top card turned out to be a deuce, but Corbett winced even before he turned up the next card. It was an ace, giving the man across from him aces and kings, full. But Corbett's card was the final nine. He had four, a cinch hand, since he knew the hole cards of the other players.

He covered up his hand for a moment and managed to dig his fingernail into the hole card in the position for a queen.

"Two pair bets," he said quietly.

"Damned if I'm going to be bluffed," said the monte man. "A hundred."

He put the money into the pot, leaning far over to look at Corbett's turned-down hole card. He looked satisfied.

Corbett looked thoughtful a moment, then studied his hole card and shook his head. Finally he said, "The hundred and—two hundred."

The man with the three jacks let out a roar. "He's pulled it again, that innocent business again and let us walk into it." He threw in his three-jack hand.

The man with the aces and kings looked across at Corbett. "Just you and me, and you may have four nines, but I don't think so." He dumped coins out of his leather sack. He counted out three hundred dollars in gold, but did not throw it into the pot. "You're a good poker player, stranger, but I think you're bluffing."

"Well, then, you bluff," retorted Corbett.

"I don't have to." He looked across the blanket, trying to count Corbett's money. "How much you got there?"

"Another hundred and fifty."

"Anything back of it?"

"Nothing."

"Then I'll just raise you the hundred and fifty. That'll keep you out of mischief."

Corbett promptly threw in his money. "You lose. I've got the four."

A cry of consternation was torn from the mouth of the three-card monte man. "You're bluffing!"

Corbett turned up the fourth nine.

The three-card monte man caught up his greatly lightened sack of gold and leaped to his feet. He stood for a moment glaring down at Corbett, then whirled and strode off.

Corbett gathered in his winnings. He played for another half hour, won a few dollars more, which put him over the two-thousand dollar mark, then drew out of the game. He decided to walk toward the cabin, but was hailed by the three-card monte man, who straightened up from inside one of the lean-tos.

"What're you playin', fellas, poker?" he jibed, quoting Corbett's opening line before getting into the game. "You knew those cards were nicked!"

"Of course," admitted Corbett, "and I figured you were the lad who did the nicking the way you kept leaning across to look at the cards."

"I don't see well," grinned the three-card monte man. He looked around and lowered his voice. "You and me could team up and get rich."

"Here? The boys'd run out of money."

"Uh-uh, they get paid all the time. Everybody's money rich and no place to spend it." `

"I thought this was a hideout. How can they get money holed up here?"

The monte man chuckled. "Cattle. My share this month was over two thousand."

Corbett frowned. "More likely you went out and held up a bank."

"Uh-uh, cattle money on the hoof. Prime steers." He closed one eye. "And we don't do the rustling. The stuff is brought to us. All we do is drive it through the hills, collect and split."

"Who do you sell it to?"

The three-card monte man looked past Corbett and raised his voice. "I'll play again later, but I'm tired now."

He walked away abruptly. Corbett turned and saw that Boggs was coming toward him. "Salinger wants to see you."

"Salinger? Who's he?"

"The boss, the head man."

"I thought you were the big fella."

"I take my orders from Salinger. Get on your horse and trot over there as quick as you can."

"Isn't he here?"

"Next valley. Six, seven miles. We're only the outpost here. Salinger's place is the main camp."

"How'd he know I was here?"

" 'Cause I sent a man to tell him while you were sleeping. It's the rule. And a word of advice to you. I'm a softhearted slob. You can make your jokes with me, but don't try any of that on Salinger. He'll eat you for dinner without bothering to cook you. Catch on?"

Corbett nodded and went to his horse. He mounted, set off at a trot, following the well-worn trail that ran through the valley, up the slope in the west.

As he rode he saw that there were many steers grazing

here. He slackened his speed, managed to ride closer to the animals and began looking for the brands. The wolf-head brand of Sam Forest was prominent. He counted the number of the brands. There were H-Bar-H brands, quite a number of them. There were also a few Lightning brands, which Corbett guessed were Holderman beeves, having seen a number of them on his first ride out to the Holderman Ranch. There were also one or two brands with which Corbett was unfamiliar. Of the three main brands, he counted a total of sixty-six head: twenty-two Wolf brand, thirty-six H-Bar-H and eight Lightning.

Since the Wolf Ranch and the Holdermans' were closest to the badlands, one would have thought that their brands would be the easiest to rustle. Actually the H-Bar-H Ranch was the farthest away of the three, yet its percentage of rustled steers was the largest.

Chapter Sixteen

Corbett kept his mount moving steadily and was soon riding down the western slope of the next range. As he got lower to the floor of the valley he began to see signs of the main camp and, when it was fully exposed, he saw that there were four regular log cabins and fifteen or twenty lean-tos and sheds. One of the log cabins seemed to be a store.

Corbett headed toward the store. He saw more than a dozen humans as he rode forward and knew that there would be many more in the vicinity.

A man standing on the porch of the store building watched Corbett approach, then went inside. He reappeared in a moment, followed by a man no more than forty, a tall, lean man. As Corbett approached, he saw that the man wasn't as lean as he appeared. He was exceedingly well-built and the muscles strained at his shirt sleeves.

Corbett dismounted near the store and moved toward the porch. "Salinger? I'm Jim Corbett. Boggs said you wanted to see me."

"Boggs didn't give you the best of it, said you were a windbag."

"I guess that's what he wanted me to be," said Corbett, smiling thinly.

"Where you from?"

"Last three years I've been in Montana. I got fed up dodging Indians for twenty-one dollars a month."

Salinger nodded. "Thought you looked like a soldier. What's this story you told Boggs?"

"That part's true enough. I hit a place called San Jon and the marshal threw me in the clink on a vag charge. Turned out he wanted somebody to do some free work. I don't like to work for free, so when he came in to feed me, I banged him a couple and lit it out."

"You waited long enough to rob the store."

Corbett shrugged.

"How'd you hear about this place?"

"There was another man in the calaboose."

"Why didn't he go with you?"

85

"He was only doing ten days and he was about sixty-five. Besides, I didn't want to move as slow as he would have had to travel."

"How long did you stay over in Seven Oaks?"

"I didn't. It was too big and I went through at night."

"Where are you headed for?"

Corbett hesitated and Salinger watched him carefully. Finally Corbett said, "What's on the other side of the mountains?"

"Nothing. Two hundred miles of desert."

"No towns?"

"Some Indian reservations and Fort Miller."

"Oh-oh," said Corbett. He drew a deep breath. "Maybe I'll just stay here awhile and get some rest." He suddenly grinned. "I can earn my keep. I already won two thousand in a poker game. Fella marked the cards and I discovered the marks."

"That'd be Mechem. He may wind up the richest dead outlaw in the country. Somebody's going to kill him sooner or later." Salinger nodded carelessly, then suddenly said, "How much of what you've told me is the truth?"

"Most of it."

"But not all?"

Corbett shrugged, then exhaled. "There was a little trouble in Montana. I didn't exactly get discharged from the Army."

"I thought it had to do with that when I mentioned Fort Miller. But it wasn't just Army trouble, was it?"

"Well, yes and no."

"What was it?"

Corbett made no reply. After a moment Salinger made a gesture of dismissal. "I'd prefer you camp down here somewhere. Anywhere's all right, just so you're around when I want you."

Corbett wandered around the tiny outlaw village for awhile. A card game was going on near one of the lean-tos, but he was not interested. He found a cottonwood tree some fifty feet from the farthest lean-to and decided to settle down by it.

He took the blanket roll off his horse, unsaddled the animal and, attaching his lasso, staked it out so that the horse could graze. He lay down under the tree, using the blanket roll for a pillow.

Chapter Seventeen

It was shortly after nine o'clock when Julie Forest rode up to the Seven Oaks Hotel. She tied her horse to the rail and went into the hotel.

She nodded to Gregson and headed for the stairs.

He said, "He's gone."

She stopped abruptly. "What do you mean, *gone?*"

"He checked out. Moved. Last night."

"That's impossible," cried Julie. "He—he could scarcely move."

"He moved well enough to pistol-whip Eben Smith last night. And he was moving like hell when he rode out of town."

For a moment Julie stared at Gregson in utter astonishment. Then she said softly, "Eben Smith!" She whirled suddenly and dashed out of the hotel.

On the street she sent a look toward the courthouse-jail, but hurried on to the Brady store. Jeff Brady was not in the store at the moment, but Cathy was waiting on a customer. She said something to the woman, then left her and came hurriedly forward.

"Cathy," exclaimed Julie, "it's true what I just heard? That Jim Corbett pistol-whipped the deputy?"

Cathy nodded. "I'd have given ten dollars to have seen it. Dad was there. He said it was something he'd never seen in his whole life. Mr. Corbett faced down Eben, dared him to draw his gun, then beat him in the face with his own gun. Dad says Eben's nose is broken, his jaw's all messed up and he—he bled like a stuck pig."

"But how could he ride out of town?" asked Julie. "When I saw him yesterday morning he couldn't move a muscle."

"He must have had a quick recovery then, because he certainly left Seven Oaks lickety-split!" Cathy bobbed her head, then suddenly gave Julie a peculiar look. "I wish *my* boy friend acted like that about *me*."

"That's nonsense," said Julie. "I've only known Mr. Corbett two days . . ."

"Oh, it's *Mister* now. It was Jim a minute ago. And if it wasn't because of you, why did he attack Eben Smith?"

"I don't know," said Julie. "I can't understand it. Not his leaving. I didn't think he would do that." A wild thought struck her. "Perhaps he didn't leave."

"Oh, he left town all right," said Cathy. "Enough people saw him. He headed west and he's probably through the mountains by now."

A frown creased Julie's forehead. Her eyes went to the woman customer who seemed to be becoming impatient. "You're busy, Cathy, I'll talk to you later."

She left the store. The Brady brothers, Cathy's father and Link, the sheriff, were standing in front of the courthouse now. They saw Julie and stopped talking to watch her, but she went on toward her horse tied in front of the hotel.

She mounted it, rode away from the hotel, then suddenly sent the animal into a swift run that became a gallop after a rod or two.

She kept the horse at a full gallop to the turn leading to the H-Bar-H Ranch and only eased off once or twice before riding into the ranch yard of the Hubbard spread.

She dismounted near the house, throwing the lines over the animal's head, then sending a quick look around, decided to try the house for Mrs. Hubbard.

Alice Hubbard opened the door as Julie's hand was raised to knock.

"Julie," she said, "how nice to see you." Then her eyes went to the panting, heaving horse. "Something's happened?"

"It's Jim—Jim Corbett. He was half-dead yesterday from the beating the Holdermans gave him, but last night, well, he had a fight with Eben Smith, then left Seven Oaks." She sent a quick look over her shoulder. "Nobody seems to know where he's gone, but I—I thought he might have come here."

"Here?"

Alice Hubbard's eyes narrowed, then she stepped aside. "Come in, Julie."

Julie went into the house. In the living room Alice Hubbard said quietly, "I went to see him yesterday afternoon. I suppose Gregson told you and that's why you asked if he was here?"

"No, Mr. Gregson didn't tell me you'd been to see him. It's just—excuse me, Mrs. Hubbard, I know I'm taking advantage of you, but I haven't got anybody to talk to and I'm worried. I—I talked to Mother yesterday and—" she stopped, bewildered. "I'm sorry, it seems so ridiculous now."

"Tell me about it, Julie," said Mrs. Hubbard.

"Well, it's just that I thought Mr. Corbett looked so—so

familiar and then Mother said something about you that I . . ."

"What did she say?"

"Just that you'd been married once, before Mr. Hubbard, and—well, she thought there'd been a son . . ."

Alice Hubbard said quietly, "You saw the family resemblance?"

Julie inhaled softly, sharply. She stared at Mrs. Hubbard.

Alice Hubbard nodded. "Yes, Jim Corbett is my son."

Julie blurted out, "Does he know you're his mother?"

"I'll tell you the story, Julie," said Alice Hubbard. "No one knows it that I know of, and I—I wouldn't ever have told it to anyone. Except that Jim came back."

She paused while her memory groped through the mists of time. "My father had a small business in Brownsville at the time of the trouble with Mexico. It wasn't a very good business, but we managed to get by. The town filled up with soldiers and there was a lot of sickness. Yellow fever, malaria. My father got sick and before I even realized how sick he was, he died. I was left alone—I scarcely knew my own mother. She had died when I was a child and there was only my father and me. I couldn't run the business. The physical effort was too much for me; it was a lumber business. I'd met Mr. Corbett two or three times. He was a farmer living about ten or twelve miles from Brownsville. He was there when—when my father was buried and he told me that he needed a wife to help him with the farm. I was only seventeen and it seemed like the answer to my problem. I married him. I didn't love him at the time, but that came later." Mrs. Hubbard's voice rose, became firm and clear. "I was eighteen when Jim was born.

"It was a poor farm and dry farming was impossible. My husband worked from dawn till after dark. I helped him. There was never enough of anything, but we kept at it. Then, when Jim was five years old, Mr. Corbett died . . ."

Her voice became lower, flat. "Some people said that I married Tom Hubbard because I couldn't afford to pay a hired man. That isn't altogether true, but I couldn't do the work alone and take care of a small child. Believe me, Julie, I have thought of that many, many times through the years and I don't *think* I married Tom Hubbard just because I had to have a hired hand and couldn't pay for one."

She paused, then turning, walked to the window. After a moment she began talking again, but a harshness had come into her voice.

"We had no children, Tom and I, although Tom wanted so badly to have a son of his own. He was not a good father to

Jim, although I thought at the time that the child resented Tom. Certainly he was never responsive to him the few times that Tom showed any signs of affection. At best it was a truce between them, but it wasn't even that as Jim grew older. Hoeing corn, planting potatoes, ploughing—it isn't easy work for a grown person. It was hard on little Jim. I will say this for Tom, he never shirked work himself, but he was impatient with others. He struck Jim now and then. When Jim grew older he would run away, hide for hours, sometimes even for a day or two until hunger made him return.

"The last time was when Jim was fourteen. Tom struck him, it was just a slap in the face, but Jim attacked Tom, punched him in the face. Tom picked up the thing that was nearest to him, a pitchfork, and struck Jim once or twice with the handle.

"Jim ran away that night. That was twenty years ago. I never received a letter from him. I did not know if he was alive or dead. We lived in Texas for another two years. Finally, after a summer and a winter, when not a drop of rain fell, we decided to go elsewhere, find a place where we could make a living—exist. After we settled here, I wrote to the postmaster at Brownsville, to several of the business firms. I gave them our new address, told them if Jim—or anyone else—wrote or asked for our whereabouts, to tell them." She paused. "I guess Jim hated us so much by that time that he never went back."

She turned and faced Julie Forest. "That's the whole miserable story, Julie. I think of when he was a boy and see the face of a stranger now. I don't know Jim Corbett. I know nothing of what he's done these past twenty years. I don't know the kind of man he is. When he came here the day before yesterday I thought he was a—well, one of the kind of men I've been hiring lately. A gun fighter." She shook her head. "I'm not convinced that a detective is much better than that."

"But you went to see him yesterday," reminded Julie.

"I'm still his mother, regardless of what *he* thinks of *me*. And he didn't spare me yesterday or the day before. He's an extremely hard man, Julie. A dangerous man."

Julie found that she was breathing heavily, that she was more agitated even than she had been in Seven Oaks when she had learned that Corbett had left—and the reason for it.

She said to Mrs. Hubbard, "Do you know what kind of a man Eben Smith is, Mrs. Hubbard?"

She nodded. "A cold-blooded killer. I think he has the reputation of being one of the fastest gun fighters in the country."

"Yet Jim, as badly injured as he was himself, went up against him. Dared him to draw, then—then pistol-whipped him in full sight of a roomful of people. He—he did it because he'd found out that Smith had struck me earlier in a—a quarrel we'd had at Brady's store. Smith said some things to me that I don't think he had any right to say and I slapped his face. He struck me and was twisting my arm when Mr. Brady stopped him—with a shotgun. But that's why Jim went up to him—and he hardly knows me. At least, not that way."

Alice Hubbard said, "This Eben Smith, wasn't he a famous desperado and gun fighter before he became a deputy sheriff?" The emotion drained out of her voice. "We don't know, do we, Julie, that Jim Corbett wasn't an even deadlier gun fighter and killer than Smith before he became a detective?"

Chapter Eighteen

Barney McCorkle was sitting on a sawbuck near the house, whittling on a stick of wood. He gave Julie a careless look as she rode past him to the nearest corral.

Julie unsaddled her horse, throwing the saddle over the top corral pole. Then she turned the horse into the corral. Closing the gate, she started for the house.

Barney McCorkle stepped down from the sawbuck and blocked her direct passage. "If you haven't stopped ranching, would you be interested to know that we lost three hundred head of cattle last night?"

Julie exclaimed, "We can't afford that! What have you done about it?"

"What am I supposed to do?" asked Barney. "Your mother's in the house acting the suffering widow and you're running back and forth to town, hobnobbing with detectives. Nobody's paying any attention to what's going on here."

"That's your job, isn't it?"

"It is, if I'm the foreman, but *am* I the foreman? Is anybody asking me what to do, or even interested?"

"I'm very much interested and so is mother and you know it. But I resent those remarks you've just made, the suffering widow and—what you said about me. If you want to remain here, on this ranch, you're going to have to change your tune, Barney McCorkle. I'm not going to put up any longer with that filthy tongue of yours and neither is Mother."

Barney McCorkle threw away the stick he had been whittling. "Then pay attention to what's ranch business. Come out to the western sections and I'll show you *how* they're robbing this ranch blind and I might even show you *who's* doing it. Which is more, I'm sure, than your detective has done, or is going to be able to do."

Julie regarded the foreman coolly. "I'm going inside and get an early lunch, then I'll go with you and see what you've got to show me."

She turned, walked away from McCorkle. Viciously, McCorkle threw his open knife at the ground. It buried itself in the ground, halfway up the haft.

When she came out of the house an hour later, Julie found that her horse was saddled and waiting for her. McCorkle's mount was also ready, as was that of his special crony, Hardee, the hired gunhand.

They mounted and left the ranch at an easy canter, heading west, but after a couple of miles, Barney led the way off at an oblique angle. To have continued straight ahead would have taken them over the Holderman Ranch.

As they reached rougher ground, McCorkle let his horse fall back so that he was riding abreast of Julie. He said, "You been seeing a helluva lot of this detective fella; you think he's going to find the man killed your father?"

"No," said Julie, "he has left."

"I heard that he had a ruckus in town last night, but I didn't hear that he lit out. For good?"

"I don't know if it's for good. I just know that he's not in Seven Oaks now. Please—I don't want to talk about him."

"Maybe we *ought* to talk about him," said McCorkle. "I thought it was a mistake when your father sent for a detective."

"You didn't know," exclaimed Julie, "so how could you know it was a mistake?"

"I knew," said McCorkle.

"You *couldn't* have known. Dad told Mother that not a soul but herself knew it. It was because—well, he'd found out something that had made him suspicious . . ."

"Suspicious of what? He knew we were losing stock."

"He knew, too, that someone was trying to kill him. Someone—whose identity surprised him."

"Now don't tell me that was me," snapped McCorkle.

"Was it, Barney? *Was* it you?"

"You've got a rough tongue, Julie," said McCorkle balefully. "You always did have and I made up my mind once we was married . . ."

"We're never going to be married, Barney," said Julie. "Of that you can be sure. Absolutely sure."

For the second time within twenty-four hours a man struck Julie Forest. Suddenly jerking his horse up beside Julie's, Barney McCorkle reached out and gave her a backhanded blow in the face. It was a vicious blow and knocked Julie backward so that her feet came out of the stirrups. She tried wildly to cling to the saddle, but was unable to do so. She went down to the rocky ground, landing heavily on her shoulders. For an instant the breath was knocked from her body, but then she started struggling up to her feet.

McCorkle was off his horse then. He grabbed her arms, slipped down his hands and locked her wrists together. Julie

93

tried to struggle, but the pain of her fall, as well as Barney's strength, was too much for her.

"You little fool," raged Barney, "you couldn't let well enough alone, could you?"

"You're through, Barney. You can go back to the ranch and get your things and leave. Before evening."

"Hardee," called McCorkle to the gunman, "bring your rope. I'm going to teach this little heifer a lesson that she'll never forget as long as she lives."

"Don't you dare do anything more," gasped Julie. "If you hurt me again I'll go to the sheriff. I'll swear out a warrant for your arrest . . ."

"Ah, hell," snarled McCorkle, "you don't know what this is all about." The gun fighter came trotting up with his lasso. McCorkle indicated with his head and Hardee began twisting the rope's end about Julie's wrists. McCorkle helped and in a moment her wrists were lashed firmly and McCorkle was holding the end of the rope.

"We're gonna take a little trip, Miss High and Mighty Forest. You're going to pay a little visit to some people, some of whom ain't seen a woman in quite a spell. Maybe you'll appeal to one of them because you certainly don't to me."

"You killed my father," said Julie coldly.

"I didn't," said McCorkle, "but I got me a awful good idea who did—but I ain't gonna give you the satisfaction of knowing. You'll have enough trouble of your own to keep you busy in just a little while . . ."

He yanked suddenly on the rope that held Julie captive. He half pulled, half dragged her to her horse where Hardee caught hold of her and lifted her into the saddle. McCorkle went back to his own horse, twisted the rope end about his saddle pommel and kneed his horse.

"Come on," he said to Julie, "it's time to go visitin'—up in the hills."

Chapter Nineteen

It was late in the afternoon when the pangs of hunger got the best of Corbett and he left his camp under the cottonwood and went toward the store. He entered and discovered that it actually *was* a store, although its stock was limited to food that was not readily perishable—canned goods, bacon, beans, flour and a few condiments. There was also a considerable stock of cartridges, both rifle and revolver.

A man with a game leg was making entries in a cloth-bound ledger. He looked up from his work.

"You're the new man," he said.

"You have this stuff freighted in?" asked Corbett.

"Uh-uh," was the reply. "I get it. Once a month."

"Suppose a man wants fresh meat?"

"We butcher a steer every other day."

"What do you get for fresh meat?"

"You work for it."

Corbett cocked his head to one side. "Doing what?"

The storekeeper shook his head. "Ask the boss."

"Where is he?"

"Around."

Corbett grimaced. "You don't talk much, do you?"

"I got a stiff leg, I can't run and I don't ride so good. So I do what I have to do and I don't talk about it."

"All right," said Corbett. "I'll have a couple of those cans of peaches, one of tomatoes and I'll take a chunk of that lean bacon. Four-five pounds."

"No flour?"

"I'm not much on making bread," said Corbett.

"Me neither, but I got some biscuits in the oven for supper. You can have some of them." He sniffed. "Fact is, they're ready now."

He limped into a rear room. Corbett heard the banging of a stove door, some rattling around, then the man came back. "They'll be cooled off in a minute."

He got Corbett's purchases together, then went out into the kitchen and returned with a tin plateful of biscuits. "Say, those smell good," exclaimed Corbett. "Look good too."

95

"You gonna pay or charge? Five dollars if you pay cash, ten if you charge."

"That's kinda high, isn't it?"

The storekeeper shrugged. "I'm throwing in the biscuits free."

"Well, that'll help." Corbett tossed a ten-dollar gold piece to the rough counter.

The storekeeper fished in a till and finally brought out five silver dollars. Corbett made no move to pick them up. "Don't you carry any, ah, wet goods here?"

"No sir," declared the storekeeper promptly. "That's one thing you won't find anywhere in this camp. On account of Salinger won't allow it. He's a teetotaler and he catches you drunk, or even sees you drinking, wham, you're on your way out." He grinned a little. "Nobody worse about likker than a former drunk. You heard about Salinger?"

"No," said Corbett, "tell me."

"Story's that he used to be a preacher back east somewhere—a preacher who liked his likker straight. Then he killed a man while he was drunk and had to go on the dodge. He swore he'd never drink a drop again for the rest of his life and he wouldn't have nothin' to do with people that did."

"Then how come you're chewing cloves?" asked Corbett.

"What? Me?" The storekeeper scowled. "I like cloves. Chew cinnamon sometimes."

"Sure," said Corbett, "there's nothing wrong with that. But where do you keep your private stock?"

Even though they were alone in the store, the storekeeper looked furtively around. "I got lumbago," he said, "and a bad stomach. Dyspepsia. I need a little nip now and then to keep me going." He gathered up the five silver dollars, put them into the till, then went to a flour barrel. He reached in, dug deep and came up with a pint bottle, which he wiped off on his trousers.

"Salinger sees you with this, you tell him you brung it with you, you hear?"

"I've got a better idea," said Corbett. "I'll drink it tonight, then he won't know about it."

"Stick it in your pocket!"

Corbett unbuttoned a button of his shirt, stuck in the bottle, then gathered up his purchases. "I'll be back for the cloves later."

Corbett went back to his camp. The sun was setting as he built a small fire and cut slices of bacon into the frying pan he took from his blanket roll. He fried the bacon, ate it with the biscuits and topped it off with peaches. He opened the can with his knife and speared out the chunks and deposited them, dripping, into his mouth.

It was almost dark when he finished eating and he was starting to clean up when Salinger came toward him.

"Corbett," he said, "I've been thinking about you. I'm sure you know by now that most of the boys are pretty well-heeled."

"That's good," said Corbett, "because I figure to play some more poker with them."

Salinger frowned. "I'm not a gambling man myself and I'm not too happy about the boys gambling, but I figure I've got to let them blow off steam somehow and it's better than drinking."

"Some people drink, some gamble," shrugged Corbett, "and some are woman chasers."

"You've always got an answer," retorted Salinger curtly. "I'm not so sure that I should even let you stay here. There's only room for one boss and that's me. Keep it in mind, Corbett. You try to undermine me or take over . . ."

"Relax, Salinger," said Corbett. "I don't figure on staying here long enough for that. I just want to rest a couple of days, then I'll hightail out of here."

Salinger looked down at Corbett, who was still crouched before the dying fire. "I'll help you make up your mind," he said finally. "We're going to make a cattle drive in a couple of days, a big one, and we can use another man."

"Whose cattle?"

Salinger made an impatient gesture. "Don't get smart."

"All right," said Corbett. "I've seen maybe fifty, sixty head in Boggs' valley, as well as here. How many people does it take to drive that many head of cattle to—where do you drive them?"

"West," replied Salinger, "and there won't be fifty or sixty head of cattle; there'll be a couple of thousand."

Corbett whistled softly. "That beef'll come from the east, eh?" He shook his head. "I'm not against the idea, Salinger. Not if the stuff is going west, but I don't think I want to go back east, not even a few miles."

"You won't have to. The stuff is brought to us. All we do is take it west from here."

Corbett nodded thoughtfully. "You've got some friends on the outside, I guess. But they're the ones taking the risk, they'll want the big cut . . ."

"Half," snapped Salinger. "That's the deal we've been working on. And *I* do the collecting. I give them half and the rest we split up—among those who make the drive. I take ten per cent off the top and the balance is split equally. You know how much money there is in two thousand head of beef? At thirty dollars a head?"

"Sixty thousand."

"That's thirty thousand for us. I take three thousand and that leaves twenty-seven thousand. We'll need about twenty men for the drive. You can earn yourself a nice piece of money—and maybe then you'll want to keep on traveling. West."

"How long a drive is it?"

"Two hundred miles."

Corbett screwed up his face in a scowl. "We drive two hundred miles and we get half, while the fellas herd the stuff up here, go maybe ten-fifteen miles and collect just as much."

"They can get themselves shot up or maybe even get their necks stretched if they get caught. There's no risk where we go. There's nothing west of here except three Indian reservations . . ."

"And that's where we deliver the cattle? Who pays the kickback to the agents?"

"What the hell are you talking about, Corbett?" snapped Salinger.

"I never knew an Indian agent yet who wasn't a thief. Why, up in Montana . . ."

"The hell with Montana," cried Salinger. "This is New Mexico."

"I'm just curious, that's all," said Corbett. "I like to know all the angles before I take on a job . . ."

"Well, you're not going to any more," snapped Salinger. "You're just a hired hand, that's all. One of twenty men. Either you go along and earn yourself fifteen hundred dollars or you can start traveling by yourself. West."

"I didn't say I wasn't taking the job. In fact I'd like to make the trip with you. Only when we get to the last Indian agency I'd like to get my money and keep moving. Like you said—west."

"You'll get it."

Salinger turned. A small cavalcade of horses was approaching the camp, headed in the direction of the store. Salinger left Corbett abruptly and Corbett, starting to kick out the last of the fire, looked toward the horsemen.

He saw then that it wasn't men alone riding the horses. There were two men, but the third rider was a woman. A rope ran from the horse of one of the men to the third horse, on which sat the woman. The rope was taut and the woman was apparently not cooperating, but was holding back her horse.

Corbett sprang to his feet as the horsewoman passed near a

98

cookfire and he got a quick look at her face. It was Julie Forest. Corbett's eyes darted from Julie to the horseman ahead of her and was sure, even though he could not see his features clearly, that it was Barney McCorkle.

Without troubling to clean his frying pan, Corbett dropped it into the spread-out blanket. He followed with the bacon. He rolled up the blanket quickly and carried it to his horse. He saddled the animal, sending a quick look over his shoulder in the direction of the store. The three saddled horses were now standing in front of the cabin nearest the store, but the riders had, without a doubt, gone into the cabin.

Chapter Twenty

Inside the cabin, Salinger, a heavy scowl on his face, was listening to the expostulations of Barney McCorkle. "Wasn't anything else I could do. I couldn't let her go home. She'd tell her ma, or that damn detective . . ."

"What detective?" asked Salinger.

"The one Sam Forest sent for before he was killed. He showed up at the funeral and he's been snooping around ever since."

"This is the first I've heard about a detective," said Salinger. "What is he, a Pinkerton man?"

"No. He's with an agency called Jarvis."

"I've heard of him. If anything, he's got a rougher bunch of people than the Pinkertons. Why haven't you people taken care of him?"

"He's slippery," replied McCorkle.

Julie said suddenly, "He licked you."

McCorkle showed sudden anger. "When I wasn't ready for him. The Holdermans roughed him up pretty good."

"Wait," exclaimed Salinger, "what does this detective look like?"

"He ain't much to look at," said McCorkle. "He's maybe thirty-five, five-feet-ten . . ."

"Six feet," interposed Julie, not knowing that she was helping the enemy.

"All right, six feet," glowered McCorkle. "Weighs maybe a hundred eighty . . ."

"And the Holdermans beat him up?" asked Salinger grimly. "How long ago?"

"Day before yesterday."

"He's here," said Salinger flatly. He went to the door of the cabin and called out, "Kirby, Donnelly . . ."

Two men came running toward the cabin. Salinger said curtly, "The new man who's camped over there," pointing, "fetch him." He turned back into the cabin. "Looks like we've got us a detective!" A gleam came into his eyes that was almost matched by that in McCorkle's eyes.

"I didn't think he'd be fool enough to come this way," said

McCorkle. "By God, he's walked right into the trap! If it's the last thing I do . . ."

"It might be," said Salinger grimly. "This is a dangerous man, McCorkle. I think he's much too tough for you—and too smart. I've talked to him and damned if he didn't almost have me believing his story. He was all banged up, but he was able to ride in here and tell me a cock and bull story . . ."

"Oh, he's a good bull thrower," conceded McCorkle, "but his lying days are over."

Outside a man came running up to the cabin. He burst into the doorway and cried out, "He's gone, lit out . . ."

"Damn," swore Salinger. "Search the camp." He whirled. "You," pointing at Hardee, "whatever your name is. Get on your horse and hightail it back to Boggs' camp. Tell him to stop the detective—warn the lookouts. Move!"

Hardee ran out of the cabin to his horse. Salinger turned back. "He's only one man, but I just don't feel good with a detective around."

"You've only shut off the way back," said McCorkle. "Nothing to keep him from going west."

"Where'll he go to? The desert? He wasn't carrying a canteen and I don't think he had time to pick one up." He shook his head. "He goes west, you got nothing to worry."

"But the drive," said McCorkle, "we'll be headed that way in a few days . . ."

Salinger shrugged. "We've made it before." He hesitated. "That widow woman, Hubbard, she's been writing to the governor about checking the Indian agents, making them get legitimate bills of sale, checking the brands. The agents do that and we're out of business. You know that."

"That's why this last, big drive is necessary," said McCorkle. "I'd like my share of it, too. Even if we get the detective." He looked at Julie. "I'll have to skip the country."

Salinger looked thoughtfully at McCorkle. "This fool stunt of yours may blow the whole thing. You can't kidnap a girl without starting a hue and cry. If she isn't found in a little while there's going to be posses looking and searching every gully and hole in these mountains. We've never been bothered much by outsiders, but the governor's watching this place now. That Hubbard woman's got him stirred up. I know that they're even appealing to Washington, D.C., the Secretary of the Interior . . ."

"We could take care of the Widow Hubbard," suggested McCorkle.

"It's too late for that. Out best chance is to make one last, big drive and make it quick. We can still sell to the Indian agents, and Fort Miller if necessary." He scowled. "You'd better start getting back. Go see," he stopped, looking quickly at Julie, then went on, "you know who. Tell him to start moving the stuff tonight the minute you see him. I want half of the herd here by noon tomorrow and the rest by evening. As much as you can and don't bother to ask questions."

"Two thousand head?" asked McCorkle. "Can you handle that many?"

"Three thousand," said Salinger. "It's the cleanup."

McCorkle started for the door and Corbett, stooped just below the window at the back of the cabin, risked a quick look through the window. He thought that they would all be looking toward the door, but Julie was turned and caught a glimpse of Corbett. A low cry was torn from her throat.

Salinger turned, looking at her suspiciously.

Julie recovered quickly. "You can't leave me tied up like this!" she cried. "It's inhuman."

"You'll make trouble," said Salinger. "My boys see you wandering around . . ."

"I'm not going to wander around. I—I'll stay wherever you tell me. Just don't keep me tied up."

McCorkle was gone. Salinger hesitated, then reached into his pocket and drew out a clasp knife. He opened the blade and cut the ropes that tied Julie's wrists together.

"I haven't got time to go chasing you around here," Salinger snapped. "Stay put now or I'll truss you up like a plucked turkey." He went to the door, looked outside, then picked out a man. "You. Here . . . !"

A man came to the door, a hulking beetle-browed man in his middle twenties, who could easily have been a strangler.

"Yeah, boss," he said, then his eyes went past Salinger and saw Julie. "Hey, ain't that somethin'!"

"You sit here in the doorway," ordered Salinger. "Keep a watch on the girl. Don't let her out. I've got some things to do, but I'll be back in a little while."

He went past the man out into the night. The big bruiser stood in the doorway, grinning wickedly as his eyes roamed over Julie.

"You and me could have some fun," he said meaningly.

"You heard the boss," said Julie. "You wouldn't dare."

"I might," said the guard. His eyes went to the window in the rear. "You could sneak out the window when he's gone to sleep."

The suggestion revolted Julie. She went to the window, then stiffened as a whisper came to her. "I've got something here," whispered Corbett from outside. "Take it when you can, then give it to the man at the door."

Julie turned, leaned against the window sill, her head and shoulders above the sill. She felt something touch her back and said loudly to the man at the door, "Why don't you sit down—in the doorway, he said, didn't he?"

The guard turned to seat himself as directed, and in the second that he was not looking at Julie, she reached around, caught the flask of whisky that was held to her.

She lowered her hands, the bottle held behind her. The man at the door had seated himself. Julie walked toward him.

"I've got something here," she said, "only—promise you won't take it all . . ."

She brought out the pint of whisky. The man gasped in delight. "What the hell! Who'd ever have thunk it?" He scrambled to his feet, snatched the bottle from Julie, then moving behind the door where he could not be seen from outside, tilted the bottle to his mouth and let the fiery liquid gurgle into his stomach. He drank a quarter of the bottle without stopping for breath. Then he lowered the bottle and looked at Julie with admiration. "You're a woman after my own heart," he said. He extended the bottle to her. "Here."

"No, I had a drink a little while ago," replied Julie. "There was another bottle . . ."

"Then down the hatch," exclaimed the stocky man, tilting the bottle up to his mouth again.

He was still gurgling down the whisky when Salinger appeared in the doorway. He stopped dead in his tracks. "Hurley, you miserable specimen of humanity, I've barely turned my back on you and . . ."

Hurley tore the bottle from his mouth, choked when he saw Salinger and thrust the bottle at Salinger. Salinger knocked it from Hurley's hand and the flask crashed against the wall, wasting more than three dollars' worth of whisky at the price Corbett had paid for it.

Hurley realized his plight then. He pointed at Julie. "She gave it to me!"

Salinger struck the hulking man in the face with his open hand. It was a hard, stinging blow and Hurley cowered back. "She did!" he howled. "She gimme it . . ."

Salinger hit the man again. "You lie in your teeth," he snarled. "I just untied her hands a few minutes ago. She wasn't carrying anything at all."

"She got it here then," cried Hurley.

Salinger swung again at Hurley, this time with his fist, but the bruiser sidestepped and rushed for the door. Salinger leaped after him, letting go with a mighty kick.

It was at that moment while Salinger's back was turned that Corbett came through the window. Salinger turned back, saw Corbett coming toward him, his revolver in hand pointed at Salinger's stomach.

"Corbett," said Salinger, "I should have known . . ."

"Close the door, Julie," ordered Corbett.

She moved quickly, going behind Salinger to shut the door.

"Put it down," said Salinger. "You haven't got a chance."

"Neither have you," retorted Corbett.

"Shoot," said Salinger, "and you won't get fifty feet from this cabin."

"Get his gun," Corbett said to Julie, but without taking his eyes off Salinger.

Julie moved up behind Salinger, but as she reached for the outlaw leader's weapon, Salinger went for the gun. Julie's clutching hands grabbed his, clung to it. Salinger tried to shake Julie off him. "You're fools, both of you," he raged.

Then Corbett was before him. Salinger saw the upthrown gun arm of Corbett, tried to dodge the blow, but could not. Corbett's gun smashed against the side of his head and, as he fell, the weight of his body tore Julie's hands clear of their desperate grip.

Corbett stooped, took a quick glance at Salinger, then straightened and faced Julie. "We've got a few minutes, not much more," he said. "Don't waste time talking . . ."

He holstered his gun, caught Julie's arm and propelled her to the small window. He picked her up, deposited her feet first through the window and let her drop to the ground outside. He followed, clambering through the window.

Outside, he took her arm. "My horse is back here . . ."

Julie went quickly with him into the darkness, away from the lights of the cabin and that coming from the rear of the store.

They came to his horse within a hundred feet. It was tied to a bush, but Corbett released it quickly. "I'll have to lead him. For awhile, at least."

With Corbett leading, they started on a wide circle away from the cabins and lean-tos. As long as Salinger remained unconscious they were all right. A man had gone to Boggs' camp but that was several miles away. There would be no returning riders for some time. Corbett intended to use that time.

Chapter Twenty-One

A few minutes later, with the campfires mere flickering dots in the darkness, Corbett mounted his horse. He reached down, gripped Julie's arm firmly and half lifting her, helped her vault up on the horse behind him.

He turned the horse to the south and soon picked up the trail that led from Salinger's camp to the eastern outpost of Boggs'. Corbett wanted to get through the pass before meeting anyone, either returning to Salinger's place or sent there by Boggs. The second valley would be difficult enough to negotiate.

He put the horse into a swift, steady run. He knew the limits of the animal from long association with it and he did not think the double load would wear it down for some time.

In ten minutes they were through the pass, looking down upon Boggs' camp, lighted by spots of fire. Corbett had taken his bearings in daylight and knew that the trail ran directly between the various lean-tos and that it was therefore incumbent upon him to circle the lights entirely.

Corbett tried to do that, riding as far to the north as possible, but the valley was not that wide and he could never get more than two or three hundred yards from the fires. However, that was enough as long as the moon did not rise, and he knew from the previous nights that it would be late in rising. The stars, however, began to come out and they created enough light to cause him concern.

He slackened the speed of the horse and they passed the camp. Soon they were climbing again and the valley narrowed. Corbett had been thinking about that and he finally came to a decision. He stopped his horse and let Julie to the ground, then dismounted himself.

"They'll be expecting us to try to force the pass," he said. "They know how much start we have and they can time us pretty well. I don't think we can make it. Not now."

"But what can we do?" exclaimed Julie softly. "We've got to get through and warn Mother and the ranchers."

"McCorkle's through by now," said Corbett. "If he goes back to the ranch and sees you coming home, he's going to be pretty desperate. I think we should find a hole and crawl into it until morning. Then I'll be able to see what we're in and try to figure out something."

"Mother's going to be awfully worried," said Julie. "She has no idea of what's happened to me, but if I'm not home —" she stopped.

Corbett said, "You came through the pass, you know what it's like. You want me to force it—with people shooting at us from both sides?"

"No," said Julie.

Corbett found her arm in the darkness and gripped it firmly. Leading his horse with the other hand, he started carefully forward. He was bearing steadily east, but trying to keep as far to the northern side of the valley as possible in spite of the rough ground.

They had been going steadily for a few minutes and Corbett was aware that they were climbing. Suddenly he saw a black path on the left and turned toward it. It was no more than a tiny coulee that went into the mountain for perhaps fifty feet and was heavily covered with brush.

Corbett forced a way through the brush, then tied the horse's reins to a sapling. "I think this is as good a place as any," he told Julie. "It might be a good time to catch some sleep. I'll keep watch."

"I couldn't possibly sleep," said Julie.

It was pitch black inside the brush but, guiding himself by touch, Corbett unstrapped the blanket roll from his horse and dropped it to the ground. He found Julie in the darkness and urged her to sit down.

Corbett remained standing, straining his ears for they were the organs upon which he must now depend. Sight was completely gone. After awhile he thought he heard the drumming of a horse's hoofs, then again the clatter of at least three or four galloping horses. They died out, however, and the silence around them became heavy.

Their eyes became used to the darkness and he was able to make out Julie, seated on the ground, her back against the blanket roll.

She said suddenly, "I talked to your mother today."

She could not see his reactions in the darkness, but he remained silent so long that she felt it necessary to continue. "I've always liked her. She's a fine woman."

"Did she tell you?" he asked finally.

"No, I—I guessed. That is, Mother and I both. I mentioned the facial resemblance and then Mother said that years ago, when they saw much more of each other than in recent years, your mother had told her she had been married before."

Corbett made a hissing sound with his lips. Julie stopped talking but heard nothing. It took her a few moments to realize that Corbett had merely cautioned her to stop her from talking about his mother.

After about ten minutes Corbett said, "I've got some food in the roll if you'd like to eat."

"I'm not hungry," Julie replied shortly. After a moment she added, "I think I'll try to sleep, after all." She moved down, stretching out so that her head alone rested upon the blanket roll.

Corbett remained standing near his horse, but when another fifteen or twenty minutes had passed without Julie speaking again, he lowered himself quietly to the ground.

He said quietly, unemotionally, "I guess she told you that I ran away from home when I was fourteen."

Julie made no reply, but he was aware that she was not breathing heavily and that she was awake. He continued, "I walked and I got some rides and I slept whenever I got too tired to walk. I didn't get too much to eat and in about two weeks I got to Westport Landing. I managed to get on a boat going to St. Louis and after we were one day out they found me. Since they were short of deckhands, the captain put me to work and I got to St. Louis. I did whatever I could in St. Louis, but it wasn't good. I shined shoes and ran errands, I sold newspapers and I worked on the docks. Sometimes I ate once a day, sometimes not at all. I slept in alleys or under the docks and after two years the war began and everybody was enlisting in the Army. I was under sixteen but the recruiting officers weren't too particular. I was still a couple of months short of seventeen when our army was at a place called Shiloh. That's when I stopped being a youth." Corbett exhaled heavily. "The Army was my home until three years ago."

"Three years ago, that was '76," Julie said finally.

"That was when I decided I'd had enough of the Army," said Corbett. "Right after the Little Big Horn. I was with Major Benteen's battalion, but I could just as well have been with Custer two miles away. I'm here now because Benteen liked his whisky better than he liked fighting. My time was up and I did not re-enlist. I went to Chicago and became a detective. The pay was a lot better than it was in the Army. After fifteen years in the Army, I was drawing a sergeant's pay. I was never an officer because I hadn't had enough school, although I did try to get some education after the war. By reading books." He stopped, then made a gesture

107

that he knew she could not see in the darkness. "That's about all there is to it."

Julie said, "You never wrote to your mother in all those years?"

"In those first years I was too bitter, and after Shiloh there didn't seem to be much point to anything. It was enough of a job to live from day to day."

He paused. "After the war, two or three years after, I had a thirty-day furlough. I went to Texas. There wasn't much left of our house and the farm was a great big patch of sand."

"Your mother wrote to the post office in Brownsville," exclaimed Julie. "She gave her new address. She even wrote to a number of the stores and business firms. When they left there, they didn't know where they would find a place to settle down and she didn't think the few neighbors you had would be able to stick it out. She thought sure you would go to Brownsville, which had become a big town by then . . ."

"As far as I'm concerned," said Corbett, "my mother died twenty years ago and now, if you're not going to sleep, *I'm* going to catch a little. I didn't sleep much last night and I've got to be alert tomorrow morning."

She heard his body touch the ground as he threw himself down and she turned on the blanket roll to seek him out, but she saw him turned away from her a few feet away, and she remained silent.

She slept.

How long she did not know. It might have been five minutes and it might have been five hours. When she opened her eyes, she saw the moon between branches of the brush overhead. It was high in the sky and almost full and she could see Corbett quite well.

He was standing again near his horse, his left arm draped over the saddle.

Julie said, "Have I been asleep very long?"

"Long enough," he replied.

"Have you any idea what time it is?"

"I've got a watch," he said, "but I don't think I could read the time on it. It's about an hour until dawn."

"If you kept track of the time you didn't really sleep, did you?"

"I spent enough nights awake in the Army," he said. "I can pretty well judge the time. I think we ought to eat something now."

"Of course, if you wish . . ."

She moved away from the blanket roll and he got down on his knees and undid it. He found the bacon, cut off some

108

thick slices. He handed one to her, as well as one of the two remaining biscuits that he had kept from his meal the evening before.

"There's no water," he said, "but I've got a can of peaches here. And one of tomatoes."

He cut open one of the cans. It turned out to be the peaches and he removed the top of the can completely and handed it to her. "Drink the juice if you don't want the peaches."

"I happen to like peaches," she said.

He opened the can of tomatoes and they finished off both of the cans, passing them back and forth, so that both got some of each can.

When they were finished eating, Corbett sat cross-legged near her. "I don't know what we're going to run into in the morning so I thought we might as well talk . . ."

"You mean in case something—happens—to *you* and I pull through!"

"That isn't what I meant," he said irritably, "and stop trying to find noble motives in me. I'm a detective. My agency's being paid and I get paid by them. You heard Salinger, the leader of the outlaws. They're going to sweep the ranches tomorrow. They'll pretty well clean off the Forest Ranch because it's the closest ranch and they're in a hurry. You know that McCorkle's in on it and probably some of those fancy gunhands he's hired for the Forest Ranch. But he isn't the leader . . ."

"I know," said Julie. "Salinger almost came out with the name of the—the man who killed my father. He's the leader of the rustlers, isn't he?"

"Yes." Corbett hesitated. "I could make McCorkle talk if I could get hold of him, but he's going to be hard to catch." He paused again. "I bribed the Wells Fargo man in Seven Oaks . . ."

"Mr. Bonner?" exclaimed Julie.

"He's been tapping the till and needs money badly. I paid him a hundred dollars and he showed me a telegram that my —that Alice Hubbard sent to the Secretary of the Interior, in Washington, D.C."

"About stopping the Indian agents from buying stolen beef," said Julie.

"I was already outside the window when Salinger told that to McCorkle. What struck me at the time was how did Salinger *know* that when McCorkle didn't?"

"Bonner! He's in the pay of the outlaws!"

"No, *I* corrupted Bonner. He had a guilty conscience. Thought I'd come to Seven Oaks to investigate him. Salinger

109

didn't say anything about a telegram. He said correspondence between my mother and the governor of the state." Corbett was unaware that he had finally used the phrase, "my mother."

"Somebody's been reading her mail."

"What I'd like to know is does she take the letters to the post office herself, or does she send her mail by one of the ranch hands?"

"I'll ask her when I see her again."

"That may be too late."

"Why? Don't you think we'll get out of this?"

"The next couple of hours will determine that," said Corbett. He fell silent again, while Julie waited. Finally Corbett said, "I counted brands yesterday. There were more H-Bar-H steers than any others. The next largest number were the Wolf head . . ."

"That's ours."

"I know. What bothered me is that there were also some Holderman brands. Isn't Pete Holderman supposed to be a friend of the boys here in the hills?"

"That's what everybody in Seven Oaks has always said. I know from what my father—and mother—said that he used to live here in the hills until about sixteen years ago. He's always remained friendly with the outlaws."

"Julie," said Corbett, "I want to get one thing straightened out. You told McCorkle that I was a detective?"

"I'm afraid I did. We quarreled about you and I said something about father not having trusted him. I don't remember exactly now, but he either got it out of me, or—" Julie frowned in the darkness, "I had the feeling that he already knew you were a detective."

"That's the part that's bothered me," said Corbett. "Too many people knew that."

Chapter Twenty-Two

Helen Forest had spent a sleepless night. Julie had not come home for supper, but Mrs. Forest had not been concerned. It was unlike Julie to go off to Seven Oaks without first telling her mother, but Mrs. Forest knew of the turmoil through which Julie had been going the last couple of days, and she did not mind.

Nine o'clock came and went, then ten and Mrs. Forest became alarmed. That Julie might have gone to Seven Oaks to see after the detective had, of course, occurred to her, but she would not have remained from the middle of the afternoon through the evening. Of course she could have gone to visit with Mrs. Hubbard, but again she would not have remained late enough to cause her mother concern.

Mrs. Forest left the house, went to the corral in the darkness to see if she could pick out Julie's horse. She couldn't, of course, for one horse was pretty much like another to her. There was a light still in one of the bunkhouses and Mrs. Forest went to it.

She hesitated before knocking on the door, but it was opened by a cowboy still fully dressed; he was a middle-aged man named Jenkins who had been with the Forests for more than a dozen years.

He exclaimed when he recognized Mrs. Forest, for it was the first time that she had ever come to a bunkhouse after darkness.

"Miz Forest!"

"I'm worried, Jenkins," said Mrs. Forest. "Julie hasn't come home and I—I wondered if her horse was in the corral . . ."

"It wasn't when it got dark. I checked the corral gate the last thing and I saw that she hadn't got back yet." He hesitated, then added, "McCorkle's horse was still gone."

"She went away with him?" asked Mrs. Forest.

He nodded. " 'Bout three-four this afternoon."

"Where? In which direction did they go?"

Jenkins pointed toward the west. "Cliff Hardee rode along with them."

"Hardee? He's one of the new hands, isn't he?"

"Yes'm."

Mrs. Forest was now more concerned than before, but she did not want to reveal it. "As long as she's with Barney it'll be all right. Thank you, Jenkins, and good night."

"Good night, Miz Forest."

Mrs. Forest went back into the house and began to pace the floor. At eleven o'clock Julie had still not returned, and by twelve Mrs. Forest had become frantic.

She went outside again. The bunkhouses were all dark now, there was no sound whatever. She stood on the back porch awhile, then went down to the ranch yard.

She toyed with the idea of harnessing up the buckboard and going to town on the rare chance that Julie and Mc-Corkle might have gone there, but she discarded the idea, Julie might return at any moment.

She went back into the house, undressed for bed and actually went to bed, but she was up again within five minutes. She went back into the living room, paced the floor, then got a book and tried to read.

By one o'clock she had come to a definite conclusion. Something had happened to Julie, something—drastic. But there was nothing she could do about it. Nothing until morning.

Having reached the calamitous conclusion, Helen Forest found that a degree of calmness had come over her. In the morning she would face what there was to be faced.

She did not go back to bed, but she seated herself on the sofa and after awhile even stretched out on it. Toward morning a chill forced her to get a blanket from her bed and at five o'clock she dressed herself.

She made coffee, drank it and, before it was even full light outside, went out and walked toward the corral. Jenkins was already by the corral.

"They haven't got back, Miz Forest," he said.

"I know. I'm going to town and see the sheriff. If you'll hitch the team to the buckboard . . ."

"Yes, ma'am."

Jenkins hurried into the corral.

Five minutes later Mrs. Forest was in the buckboard starting for Seven Oaks. She had been gone twenty minutes when McCorkle rode up to the corral and dismounted.

Jenkins saw him coming and was ready. "Miz Forest just went off to town, Barney," he said. "She's worried about Julie . . ."

"Well, I'm not," snapped McCorkle.

"She rode off with you yesterday," said Jenkins, "but she hasn't come back."

"Oh, hell," snarled McCorkle. He went past Jenkins toward the bunkhouse. Jenkins hesitated, then followed.

In the bunkhouse three or four men were in the process of getting dressed. A few were still asleep. McCorkle entered, drew his revolver and fired into the ceiling.

"Rise and shine," he roared, "every mother's son of you!"

The sleepers awakened. One of them was in ill-humor. "What the hell, Barney, this ain't the Fourth of July . . ."

"It's payday," cried McCorkle. "This is what we've been waiting for. The Big Day. We're going to strip this damn ranch of every head of cattle and we're going to split the loot and get the hell out of this country."

Whoops of joy went up but, behind McCorkle, Jenkins stepped forward. "I always suspected you was in with the danged rustlers . . ."

That was as far as he got. McCorkle's gun was already in his hand. He thrust it toward Jenkins, fired once, then pulled the trigger a second time as Jenkins already lay on the floor.

McCorkle looked around. "Anybody else here ain't with us?"

No one challenged McCorkle. The men in the bunkhouse were all hands that McCorkle himself had hired within the past six months.

Helen Forest reached the town of Seven Oaks before six o'clock. There were only one or two people to be seen on the entire street as she drove her team directly to the sheriff's office. She got down from the buckboard, drew a deep breath and went to the door of the sheriff's office. She knocked on the door. There was no reply and she tried the door.

It was unlocked. Mrs. Forest opened the door and stepped tentatively into the office.

Eben Smith was seated in the sheriff's big chair behind the sheriff's desk. He was dozing, only half-awake, but he recognized Mrs. Forest instantly.

"What the hell!" he exclaimed.

Mrs. Forest decided to ignore the profane greeting. "I came in to see the sheriff."

A huge strip of adhesive tape was stretched from one side of Smith's face to the other across the bridge of his nose. A bandage ran from under his chin along the left side of his face and over his hair.

He got to his feet, sneered at Mrs. Forest and said nastily, "Link don't come down until eight-nine o'clock. When he ain't here, I'm the sheriff. Now what the hell do you want?"

Smith had gone too far and Helen Forest's concern over Julie's welfare became sublimated to a sudden anger. "First of all you can keep a civil tongue in your head or you may find yourself with the rest of your face in bandages . . ."

"I'm ready for him," snarled Eben Smith. "I'm ready and waiting and the minute I see him, he's a dead man. And you got a hell of a crust comin' in here when you're the one brought that damned detective here . . ."

Mrs. Forest turned abruptly and went through the door. She heard Smith yell after her, "And that goes for that daughter of yours. She's nothing but a . . ."

Mrs. Forest clapped her hands over her ears and did not hear the rest of it, but she knew pretty well what foul epithet Smith had yelled.

She climbed into the buckboard, turned the team and drove swiftly out of town. At the H-Bar-H turn-off, she turned left. She would wait at Alice Hubbard's until nine o'clock, by which time the sheriff would be at his office. She would return then.

Chapter Twenty-Three

The moon had dimmed because of the breaking of the dawn, but it was another half hour before Corbett ventured out of the shelter of the heavy brush. Bent low, he scudded swiftly downhill out of the coulee to where he could see the trail.

It was a good hundred yards from where he was crouched. He studied the terrain for long moments, then finally shifted to the top of the ridge and the pass that went between two banks of earth and rocks. It was perhaps two hundred yards from where he was. He focused on it for a long time and finally made out the figure of a man seated with his back against a cut in the south bank. He seemed to have a rifle across his legs.

The man was on the wrong side, however. When Corbett had made his entry into the valley he had been stopped by a man on the other side of the trail who had stepped out from behind a boulder. The man had either shifted his position or had been reinforced. Corbett was certain that it was the latter. But was there only one additional man? Or more?

Corbett remembered, too, that the man had told him he had passed a look out farther down who had not been seen by Corbett and who had not challenged him as he rode by.

The double lookouts, within shouting or shooting distance of each other, was good strategy for the outlaws, but it was damned difficult for anyone trying to enter their stronghold. And even harder for someone trying to leave it. Especially since they had been alerted.

The approaches to the pass were too difficult for a horseman. A man had to go by the trail, or be a mountain goat. No horse could climb those approaches.

He returned to Julie and explained the situation to her. "Have you got the nerve to ride up there alone?" he asked her.

"They wouldn't let me through."

"Of course not. What I had in mind was that I would go ahead, get to one of the high points overlooking the trail, then when you came along I could get the drop on them."

"What do you mean, get the *drop*? If there's more than

115

one of them you *couldn't* get the drop on two of them—in different positions. You'd have to shoot them before they shot you."

He nodded. "We'd have to make a run for it, at any rate, and there's the last man down below. Maybe more than one man. He'd hear the shooting and be ready for us."

"But it's the only way, isn't it?"

"I can't think of any other way."

"Then tell me what you want me to do."

"Give me a half hour—I'll leave my watch with you—to get into position. Then get on the horse, ride down to the trail and move up to the pass. When they stop you I'll make my play." He drew his revolver and extended it to her.

She shook her head. "I'm not very good with one. I'm better with a rifle."

He hesitated. "I thought I'd keep the rifle in case I have to shoot from a distance. But now that I think of it, that wouldn't be any good. It's got to be close up, or not at all." He nodded. "Keep the rifle."

He took out his watch and handed it to her. "A half hour. And don't ride too fast. That'll give me another five to ten minutes. I may need them." He started to turn away.

"Jim!"

He turned back.

"Be careful."

He smiled wanly and went off. His starting point was out of sight of the pass and he moved swiftly, climbing up the rather steep slope. It was rough going for the walls of the coulee were steep and there was very little growth on the slopes themselves. The hand grips were few, the footing uncertain, composed mostly of shale and gravel. There would be danger of starting a noisy landslide.

As he climbed it became even more difficult and he stopped to rest when he was still fifty feet from the top. He was still not in the best of condition after his beating by the Holdermans, and even if he had been at his finest it would still have been a hard task.

He went at it again, moving more slowly this time. There was a bush some ten feet from the top and he grasped it to give himself a bit of leverage. The bush came away and shale began clattering down the steep side. He groaned and froze against the cliff. Shale was still going down when he forced himself to move up and on.

He made it to the top and was perspiring copiously. He wanted to rest, but he knew that the best part of twenty minutes had been consumed to make the climb and he had to be in position in another fifteen minutes.

He was still several hundred yards from the pass, over one of the roughest bits of terrain he had ever encountered in the west. Within fifty yards he came to a gap that was twenty feet across. He looked down into the gap, knew that he could not descend and climb up again on the other side. He ran off to the left, hoping that the gap would narrow. It did to about a dozen feet.

There was nothing to it but to leap across it. He studied the gap carefully, then searched for the best spot for the take-off. He found it and studied the other side of the gap. He decided that the distance was possibly not more than eleven feet, perhaps a few inches less, but that it would be a difficult leap.

He shoved his revolver down as tightly into the holster as he could, then walked back a dozen feet, twenty. He drew a deep breath and started running. His eyes were on the ground for he wanted every inch available for the take-off. As he ran he increased his speed.

And then he leaped. He had one awful glimpse of the chasm below him while he was in mid-air and then his feet landed on solid ground. He threw himself forward, landing on his hands and knees. The pain that shot through his body was proof that he was still not fully recovered from his recent bruises.

But he had made the jump. He got to his feet, brushed off his hands and found that his left palm was bleeding from a cut. He wiped off the blood on his trousers, loosened his revolver in the holster and started quickly forward. Soon he heard voices and dropped to his knees. He scurried ahead on hands and knees and in a moment reached the edge of the cut. He peered down and saw Julie astride his horse just below him, not more than fifty feet from where he was perched. An outlaw was gripping the bridle reins of the horse, while just beyond was a second man holding a rifle.

There was no time for Corbett to search the area below to make sure that the two guards were the only ones on the scene, for the altercation below reached its climax at that moment. The man who was already gripping the bridle reins reached out to grab Julie and tear her from the saddle.

The rifle that Corbett had left with Julie came up from the far side and Julie struck down at the man trying to grab her. The man saw the gun coming and jerked aside. The blow Julie had launched was a complete miss and the man was tearing her down from the saddle to the ground.

Corbett fired at the man assaulting Julie. He fired instinctively, without aiming, as he had taught himself to do through the years, and his bullet went true, catching the man

117

in the back. He cried out, staggered and fell to the right. But his hold on Julie remained and she was thrown violently to the ground.

The outlaw beyond the horse, already moving forward, caught sight of Corbett and threw himself to his knees. He fired under the horse's neck, a quick snapshot that kicked up dirt inches from Corbett's face. Corbett found him then. He fired twice at the second outlaw, once to get him in the legs to bring down his upper body, then a second time as the man fell.

Julie's alertness, in spite of her own predicament, was all that saved Corbett then. Corbett had not seen the third man. He was off to the left more than fifty feet away from the scene of battle. He was behind a huge rock with a rifle lying across the top of it.

Julie, scrambling to get to her feet, sent a quick snapshot at the third man. She missed the man, but the bullet struck the boulder and bits of rock were driven into the man's face just as he was in the act of firing. His bullet went completely wild and then Corbett got him with a well-placed one.

Corbett sprang to his feet, shoved his gun into the holster and half jumping, half scrambling, went down the steep bank. He hit the ground on his hands and knees, sprang up in almost the same instant.

He rushed for his horse which had not moved during the fight, which was the way he had been trained. He leaped into the saddle, reached out for Julie.

"Come on!" he cried.

She scrambled toward him. He caught her hand, lifted, and with her own spring she got onto the horse behind the saddle. Her left arm went around his waist, held him tightly, for her right hand was still encumbered with the rifle.

Corbett sent the horse driving through the pass down the trail. A hundred yards and he bent low in the saddle. It was well that he did, for a rifle cracked ahead and to the left and a bullet went zinging by overhead.

"Down!" he shouted over his shoulder, and bent lower himself. His revolver was in his hand, but he had not yet found the hiding place of the final outpost guard.

His eyes noted a clump of brush on the left side of the trail. A flash of light struck his eyes as the sun found a piece of metal and caused the reflection.

Corbett saw the man then. He was moving out from the brush for the shelter of a tree just three or four yards away. While still at a full gallop, Corbett fired twice, the last bullets in his revolver. The first one apparently took no effect, but the second one caused the man to stumble and fall forward against the tree trunk. Corbett did not know if his bullet had taken effect on the man, causing the stumble, and he did not know if the wound, if there had been one, was a lethal one or not. He kicked his horse again and it gave forth with a final burst of speed that took it down the trail, away from the danger area.

The animal was a sure-footed one and did not stumble once in its headlong plunge down the trail. Corbett let the horse have its head and did not ease it down until it had run almost a mile. Then he gradually slackened the animal's speed until it was down to a fast walk. The horse was panting heavily from its run carrying the double load and Corbett knew that he had to stop it soon, but it was another half-mile or so before he finally halted it.

He dismounted then by throwing his leg over the horse's neck and slipping to the ground. Julie started to dismount but he gestured to her to remain in the saddle.

He stepped away from the horse, looked back up the trail. He could not see all the way to the ridge, for the trail made some turns and curves and from where he stood there were gaps that he could not survey. After a moment or two, however, he felt sure that there was no pursuit. He turned and studied the trail ahead. It was two or three miles to the range of the Holdermans and approximately the same distance to the outermost limits of the Wolf Brand Ranch.

He walked back to Julie and his mount. "We'd better rest the horse ten or fifteen minutes. Then we'll make the last run."

Chapter Twenty-Four

Going west two nights ago, Corbett had skirted the poor man's ranch of the good Holderman by almost a half-mile. He had known of his passing only by a flicker of light that he caught now and then when there were no obstructions between him and the log cabin.

Returning east, with Julie mounted behind him, Corbett had crossed the rolling foothills on Holderman property—that controlled by Old Pete and his ruffian sons. He left it, finally, when he saw the road leading up to the large Holderman Ranch. Not wanting to travel it, he cut too far to the north and, going through a patch of cottonwoods, emerged in full sight of the good Holderman's log cabin. He came closer than he had estimated he would and within a hundred yards of the cabin and ranch yard.

Someone was saddling a horse by the corral just behind the log cabin. It was a woman. She did not hear the approach of Corbett's horse until the horse was within a hundred feet of the cabin, then she whirled suddenly. She clapped her hand over her face, then realizing she was fairly seen, dropped her hands and waited defiantly for the approach of Corbett and Julie.

It was Cathy Brady.

Corbett rode up to her. He nodded as he pulled up his horse.

"Tracy around?" he asked quietly.

"He's in the house," replied Cathy. Her cheeks were flushed, her teeth were working nervously on her lower lip. She could not meet Corbett's piercing eyes and said to Julie, "I took your advice, Julie. He wouldn't make the move so I made it."

"I haven't said anything about it, have I?" asked Julie.

"We're going to be married next week," Cathy said defiantly, "and I don't give a good goddam what anyone says. In fact, I'll tell them that I came out here and spent the night."

Corbett said, "I guess that's your business—and Tracy's. I just wondered if we could borrow a horse. This one's done a

lot of work and he's getting tired of carrying a double load."
He swung his right leg over the saddle pommel and dropped
to the ground.

The house was only fifty or sixty feet away and as Corbett
approached it, Tracy Holderman came to the door. His face
was set in angry lines.

"You had to come snooping around," he said savagely.
"Well, I hope you're satisfied."

"Tracy," said Corbett, "your life's your own, yours and
Miss Cathy's, I guess. I just wanted to ask if you'd lend us a
horse. I'll return it later this morning if you wish."

"I'm not in the horse renting business," snapped Tracy. "I
own two horses and I need them both." He stopped abruptly,
his eyes going toward the corral where Cathy had moved
close to Julie, still seated on Corbett's horse. The two were
talking together earnestly. Tracy scowled. "She's supposed to
be spending the night with Julie."

"Julie hasn't been home all night," said Corbett.

Suspicion came into Tracy's face. "She's been with you?"

Corbett made a gesture of dismissal. "Mrs. Forest may
have gone to town last night looking for Julie. You might
want to know that."

"Damn," swore Tracy. "Her paw hears about that—" He
shook his head. "I don't give a damn what he says. We're
going to get married whether he likes it or not."

Corbett nodded and turned away from Tracy Holderman,
who remained standing in the doorway of his log cabin. He
walked swiftly back to his horse. As he came up, Cathy said
to him, "Julie can ride my horse. I'll borrow one of Tracy's."

Julie placed her palms upon the rump of Corbett's horse
and sprang backward, landing lightly on the ground. She ran
to Cathy's horse, mounted it quickly.

Cathy said to Corbett, "Please, Mr. Corbett, don't say anything in Seven Oaks about this."

"I'm a detective," said Corbett, "not a back-fence gossip."

Cathy flashed him a wan smile. "Tracy's overly sensitive. I
used to be myself, but I decided that I'd had enough about
worrying what people said."

Corbett mounted his horse and turned it toward the road.
He nodded to Cathy. Behind him, Julie came clattering up,
riding Cathy's horse on which the stirrups were already short-
ened.

"Goodbye, Cathy," Julie called, "and good luck!"

They passed the cabin. Tracy had gone inside. They rode
on. "What do you think of that?" asked Julie then, when they
were out of earshot of the cabin.

Corbett made no reply. Julie cast him a sideward look. "You don't approve?"

"If I were in love with a woman," said Corbett, "the last thing in the world I'd worry about is what the neighbors thought."

"But you're not in love," said Julie. Then, as Corbett made no reply, "Have you ever been?"

"I was a soldier for fifteen years. You know what soldiers do when they rush to the nearest town on payday with twenty-one dollars in their pocket."

It was Julie's turn now to flush. "That's different," she said lamely.

"It's the only kind of love a soldier can afford," said Corbett, then, aware that Julie had winced, "A married man's no good on a campaign. He's thinking of his wife, maybe his children. He's afraid to take the chances a soldier's got to take. He's a casualty figure before the shooting starts."

The harshness of Corbett's views repelled Julie and she was silent until they had turned into the road, headed for the Forest Ranch. Then she put spurs to her horse and galloped ahead of him.

Corbett followed her at an easier gait and by the time he reached the area behind the Forest home, Julie had already dismounted from Cathy Brady's horse and was running toward the house.

"Mother," she called, "I'm back."

She whipped open the door and dashed inside. Corbett heard her voice calling inside the house and, as he dismounted, a door slammed in one of the bunkhouses.

Loosening his .45 in the holster, Corbett walked toward the bunkhouse. The door blew open again from a gust of wind that seemed to be blowing through the low building. Corbett came to an abrupt stop. He looked around the ranch yard.

He knew that the Forest Ranch employed a score or more of hands, but not one was in sight. There were no horses in any of the corrals. The Wolf Brand spread could have been a deserted ranch.

Corbett drew his revolver and entered the bunkhouse. His quick look around showed him eight cots in the room, four on each side, a stove in the center of the room, but nothing living inside.

Just one dead man.

He lay on the floor near the stove. Corbett walked over to him, looked down. It was a middle-aged ranch hand. Corbett dropped to one knee, touched the dead man's face. It was

122

still slightly warm. He had been dead no more than a half hour, certainly not more than an hour.

He straightened and started back to the door, which slammed shut again before he reached it. The catch was broken on it, as if someone had slammed it open with violence when the catch was on.

He opened the door and stepped out.

Julie came running toward him from the house. "Jim," she cried, "there's no one home. I looked everywhere, but Mother's gone—" The bunkhouse door slammed shut and Julie started instinctively past Corbett to go to the house. Corbett threw out a detaining hand.

"Don't go inside!"

She stopped, stared at him in utter bewilderment and rising alarm. "What's happened, Jim?"

"McCorkle," he replied. "I guess most of the hands were his people." He jerked his head toward the door of the bunkhouses. "Except maybe one of the older hands. He's dead. Shot."

Julie gasped. "Mother!"

"No," said Corbett quickly. A beat. "You did search the house?"

"I looked in every room. But he could have taken her . . ."

"She would have been too much of a handicap. Besides," he shook his head, "he's got to work fast. You heard the orders Salinger gave him last night. My guess is your mother left before McCorkle came . . ."

Julie whirled, sending a quick look around. "The buckboard's gone."

"Then she's gone to town," said Corbett. "Probably to report that you were missing." He indicated the bunkhouse. "This happened within the hour and she was gone by then."

"You're only guessing," cried Julie. "You don't know for sure."

"If they'd killed a man here they wouldn't have let her go," said Corbett.

Julie hesitated, looking worriedly at Corbett, then turned and ran for her horse, Cathy Brady's horse. She climbed swiftly into the saddle and was headed for the road before Corbett was mounted. He followed her swiftly. They were a hundred yards or less from the main road when both saw a swiftly ridden horse going by ahead of them.

Cathy Brady returning to town. Corbett looked at his watch. It was a few minutes after eight. She would be late for her work as postmistress, he thought idly. Although her father would have long since known of her absence, especially if Mrs. Forest had arrived early in Seven Oaks.

There was little conversation between Corbett and Julie Forest as they rode toward Seven Oaks. For one thing, they were riding too fast to carry on a conversation. Julie, riding ahead of Corbett, was worrying about her mother. Corbett had his own thoughts.

He was trying to fit together bits of the puzzle that had been growing in his mind for the past two days. He had thought that he had solved the problem in his mind the night before, but there were pieces that did not quite fit. It was the larger problem that kept interfering with the small one and it was the smaller one that he was trying to solve. It was what he had been hired for.

To find the murderer of Sam Forest. The cattle-rustling did not concern him except as it crossed into the realm of the murder. Sam Forest, obviously, had learned, or begun to suspect the truth of the cattle rustling, who was behind it. At least he had been close enough for the chief rustler to try to assassinate him. The attempt had failed, but suspicion had ripened in Forest's mind. He had therefore written to Chicago for a detective to come out and apprehend the man who had tried to kill him.

Unfortunately, Sam Forest had been right. Forewarned, Forest had believed that he could stave off a second attempt on his life. He had been wrong. The murderer had caught him unawares a second time . . .

Unawares?

Sam Forest had been killed in broad daylight on a public highway within a mile of his home. Had Sam Forest been wrong in his guess as to the identity of a man who had tried to kill him and failed? The first time.

Chapter Twenty-Five

They were nearing the outskirts of Seven Oaks and Julie put her horse into a gallop and outdistanced Corbett.

Corbett entered the town at a canter. He rode his horse to the Seven Oaks Hotel and stopped. Julie was across the street, in front of the sheriff's office and courthouse. She was twisting in the saddle, searching for her mother's buckboard.

There were only a few wagons and horses on the dusty street and it was obvious to Corbett that the Forest buckboard was nowhere in sight.

Gregson, the hotel owner, came out of the hotel. "Didn't think you were coming back."

"I said I'd be back," retorted Corbett. "I'll be in and pay my bill . . ."

Julie drove her horse across the street to Corbett. "She isn't here." She saw Gregson. "Mr. Gregson, have you seen my mother in town this morning?"

The hotel man shook his head. "Can't say's I have, but then I wasn't really looking for her. She might have come and gone . . ."

A man came bursting out of the Wells Fargo office. He started running toward Corbett. It was Bonner, the agent.

"Mr. Corbett," he cried when still at a distance, "I want to talk to you . . ."

Corbett said to Julie, "She's probably gone out to the H-Bar-H Ranch."

Julie's eyes lit up. "Of course, why didn't I think of that? Are you coming out with me?"

"No," said Corbett. "There are some things I want to do here."

"You'll come out later?"

"When I've finished here."

Julie showed disappointment, but whirled Cathy's horse immediately. "Tell Cathy I'll take good care of her horse."

She went off then, at a gallop.

"Mr. Corbett," cried Bonner anxiously, "I've got to talk to you in private. It's—it's important."

"Sorry, Bonner," said Corbett, "I've no time now." He dismounted, started to tie his horse to the hitch rail. Bonner ducked under the rail, came up to him.

"Please, Mr. Corbett, the Wells Fargo investigator's here. Came in on the morning stage. I—I'm in trouble."

"That's between you and Wells Fargo," said Corbett. "'I can't help you."

"You're the only hope I've got. He's going over the books and I—I'm over five hundred dollars short."

"You were four hundred short the other day. I gave you two hundred . . ."

"I lost it, and a hundred more." Bonner caught hold of Corbett's arm. "I—I've got something important to tell you. Something really important . . ."

"It may be important to you," said Corbett, "but it isn't to me."

"It is—I'm sure of it. You'll be glad to know it."

"What is it?"

"It'll cost you—I mean, you'll give me five hundred dollars?"

Corbett let out a raucous snort. "Nothing in the world you could tell me would be worth five hundred dollars."

"But I need the money. I'm sunk if I don't have it inside of a couple of hours."

"Borrow it," snapped Corbett, "but not from me."

Bonner sent a furtive look over his shoulder and whispered, "It's from the Secretary of the Interior to the Widow Hubbard, in answer to her telegram day before yesterday." He fished a grimy telegram from his pocket, handed it quickly to Corbett and again looked over his shoulder in the direction of his office.

Corbett opened the telegram. It read:

Replying your telegram, have already communicated with Governor Walters and am today advising Indian agents to cease purchasing cattle forthwith, pending investigation by my department.

Signed: Carl Shurz,
Secretary Department of Interior

"Know what that means?" chortled Bonner. "Stolen beef won't be worth a damn and the rustling'll stop. That's worth five hundred to you."

"Not to me," snapped Corbett. "I'm not interested in the cattle rustling. I came here to find a murderer. That's all I've been hired for."

A groan was torn from Bonner's lips. "I—I got another telegram. Came yesterday. It's—it's about you, Corbett. Give me the money and I'll show it to you."

126

"Who's the telegram to?" snapped Corbett.

"Give me the money and I'll tell you."

Corbett caught the hapless Wells Fargo man by the throat. "Damn you, I haven't got time for your nonsense."

Bonner tore at Corbett's throttling hand. "You're choking me," he gasped. "Let me go—it's for you . . ."

Corbett released the man. "You've got a telegram for me and you want me to pay five hundred dollars for it? Why, you . . ."

"I don't care," sobbed Bonner, "I'm dead if you don't give me the money, so I might as well." He broke off, reached again into his pocket and produced a crumpled ball of yellow paper.

It was addressed to Corbett at Seven Oaks. The message read:

Where are you? Why have we not heard from you? Client wired this office seventeenth, canceling request. Surely you have contacted him by now and been advised. Wire immediately upon receipt.

Jarvis

Corbett stared at the telegram, started to read it a second time. Then he looked up at the waiting Wells Fargo man.

"The seventeenth! Sam Forest was murdered on the sixteenth. That means—this telegram was sent after his death—" his eyes slitted. "Who sent the telegram?"

"I don't know."

"Don't give me that!" cried Corbett. "The man who sent it is the man who murdered Sam Forest."

"I could figure that out myself last night," said the agent. "But the telegram to this Jarvis wasn't sent from here. I'm telling you the truth. The murderer wouldn't dare send it from here. He probably rode over to Roswell or some other place where there's a telegraph office."

Corbett reached into his pocket. "You can find out for me." He counted money quickly. "Here's your five hundred. Find out as quickly as you can. Wire the other offices, ask for a description of the man who sent the telegram. That's the Jarvis Detective Agency, Chicago, Illinois."

Bonner cried out in relief. "This'll save me. I'll slip it into the safe and Wexler'll never know the difference." He started for his office. "I'll let you know as soon as I get the information, Mr. Corbett. And—thanks for saving my life!"

Bonner ran to his office. Corbett started to follow, heading for the Brady Store beyond the Wells Fargo office. He had gone less than twenty feet when a voice rang out from behind him.

"Detective!" the voice cried.

A groan came from Corbett's lips. He knew who it was and nothing that had happened to him in the past few days was less desirable than what was now going to happen.

He turned. Eben Smith was coming toward him diagonally from the direction of the sheriff's office. A huge strip of adhesive plaster was stretched across the bridge of his nose and his left jaw was swollen as if he had the mumps. But there was nothing wrong with Smith's hands and that was where the danger lay.

"I didn't think you had the gall to come back," he raged.

"Hold it," cried Corbett. "I'm not looking for trouble with you."

"You don't have to look," snarled Smith. "It's found you." His right hand was swinging at his side as he continued to come forward. It was brushing the leather holster that held his revolver.

"Damn it," said Corbett, then stopped. He was facing what was probably the most dangerous man he had ever met in his entire lifetime, a man who was not only a lethal machine, but who could not be deterred from the course he had started when he had called to Corbett.

Corbett needed every resource in his body, his brain, to survive this crucial moment. That he could not stand up and outdraw the man coming toward him, he knew. Yet he could not run. There was no place to run to, even if he had wanted to do so. He had to fight and he had to fight to win—or die.

Smith was still more than thirty yards away. He would probably come another five yards, perhaps ten. Yet if Corbett made a movement he would go into action, regardless of the distance.

Corbett moved. He threw himself violently to the ground, at the same time reaching for his revolver with as much speed as he could possibly muster. His hand gripped the butt of the gun savagely, then his body smashed his hand and the gun to the ground. But Corbett kept on moving, spinning completely around. Vaguely he heard the boom of a gun. Something smashed his boot heel, kicking his foot to one side. He was on his back now. Violently he thrust out his gun and pulled the trigger and instantly cocked the hammer again. A gun boomed again and gravel was kicked into his face. Smith had missed with his second shot. The third shot would follow less than a split second later.

But there was no third shot from Smith. There was only

Corbett's second shot as he spun around to his stomach, heaved up and pulled the trigger.

Smith was falling then, and Corbett came up to his knees. He had cocked the revolver for the third shot, but it wasn't necessary. Smith was down.

Corbett got to his feet, strode forward. Smith was lying on his face. His right hand was flung out, the gun with which he was so fast was several inches from his hand. Smith was dead.

Footsteps pounded the street and voices were shouting from in front of Corbett, from behind him. He looked up, saw the heavy-set, almost middle-aged Link Brady come running toward him.

"Damn you, Corbett," raged the sheriff, "why the hell didn't you stay away?"

"He wouldn't have it any other way," said Corbett.

"Your gun," cried the sheriff. "Throw it down. You're under arrest."

"You can't arrest me, it was self-defense. These people saw it . . ."

There were at least a dozen men on the street within twenty yards of the group.

"They saw a deputy sheriff trying to arrest a man," said the sheriff grimly. "You killed an officer of the law in the performance of his duty. That's not self-defense. No judge or jury would acquit you."

"This was a personal matter between me and Smith," declared Corbett. "It had nothing to do with his job as a deputy sheriff . . ."

"That's not true. You assaulted an officer of the law the other night. You pistol-whipped him and he swore out a warrant for your arrest. Judge Pelkey issued the warrant. He was trying to serve it and you killed him . . ."

It was wrong, of course, but technically the sheriff was right. If Smith had actually sworn out a warrant for Corbett's arrest . . .

"Throw down your gun!" screamed the sheriff.

"I can't go to jail now," began Corbett. "I've got things to do."

"Shoot me," snarled the sheriff. "Shoot me in the presence of all these people and run for it and there isn't a place in the entire country where the law won't be hunting for you. For the last time, throw down that gun—or use it."

The sheriff had not drawn his own gun. He was relying entirely upon his authority. And it was an authority that Corbett could not deny.

Corbett threw his gun to the ground. Link Brady came forward, picked it up and said to Corbett, "You're using your head now, man. Maybe you can beat this in court. I dunno. But it's the only sensible thing you can do." He inclined his head, indicating the direction of the jail.

Corbett was alone. He had no allies in Seven Oaks. Not right now. He accompanied Brady to the courthouse and sheriff's office.

The sheriff's office occupied the left half of the courthouse building. The office ran across the entire front of the section. It contained two desks, a rack for rifles and a brace of shotguns and more than a hundred "Wanted" posters tacked to the walls. A barred door was in the center of the rear wall.

When they arrived at the sheriff's office, Corbett said angrily, "This is a lot of nonsense and you know it. Smith was a gun fighter, no more, no less."

"He was my deputy sheriff," said Brady stubbornly. "I know there was bad blood between you."

"He was looking for a fight the first moment I saw him," snapped Corbett. "You know I was here on a case."

"I've heard you're a detective," said Brady, "least everybody says you are, but you haven't been acting like one that I've seen. You've been throwin' your weight around from the minute I set eyes on you. You had a fight with Barney McCorkle . . ."

"McCorkle," snapped Corbett. "Right now he and his men are stripping the Wolf Ranch of stock, driving it into the badlands. Besides which, he left one dead man back at the Forest bunkhouse . . ."

"Maybe," said Brady, "but I haven't had any complaints from any of the Forests."

"We came looking for Mrs. Forest, Julie and I. She wasn't at the ranch and she wasn't here so Julie went—"

Corbett stopped. "You don't believe a word I'm telling you."

"I'm doing my job," said Brady flatly. "That much and no more." He stepped to the cell door, opened it and moved to one side. He gestured.

Corbett exploded. "Damn you, Sheriff, listen to reason. Too much is happening now for me to sit back there twiddling my thumbs . . ."

"In," said Brady, gesturing at Corbett with the latter's own gun. "I mean it, Corbett. You're a prisoner here and you're going to be treated like every other prisoner." He cocked Corbett's revolver.

Corbett went past him, although Brady took a quick step back as he approached. He went into an aisle between two rows of cells, two cells on each side.

"Last cell on the left," called Brady as Corbett entered the cell block.

The door of the cell was open. Corbett entered and Brady, still gripping Corbett's cocked revolver, followed and closed the door. He turned a key in the lock and started to back away.

Inside the cell Corbett stepped to the bars. "Wait, Brady, you've got me safe enough. Listen to what I've got to say . . ."

"I've heard enough," said Brady grimly. He went off.

"Brady," yelled Corbett desperately. "Damn you, listen to me . . ."

Brady left the cell block, closed the door leading to his office and Corbett, hearing the door slam, knew that he was wasting his breath.

Then he found himself looking across the aisle into the cell directly opposite him. A grinning man stood there gripping the bars.

"Hell, man," the grinning prisoner said, "the sheriff ain't really half bad. Wait'll that deputy of his'n shows up. That one's the goddamndest, meanest man west of the Mississippi River, bar none."

"Not any more he isn't," retorted Corbett. "I just killed him. That's why I'm in here."

The grin disappeared from the other prisoner's face. He stared at Corbett, then a low whistle came from his throat.

Chapter Twenty-Six

As Julie Forest neared the ranch house of the H-Bar-H Ranch her eyes began searching the area for a familiar buckboard and when she saw it, finally, she exclaimed in relief.

"Come on," she cried, urging her mount to greater speed.

She swept into the ranch yard at a full gallop, then had to fight the horse, unused to her style of riding, to bring it to a halt. She leaped to the ground as soon as she had the animal under reasonable control, stumbled, then rushed toward the house.

Mrs. Forest was coming out to meet her. "Mother!" Julie cried tearfully as she rushed into the older woman's arms.

"Where've you been?" exclaimed Mrs. Forest. "When you didn't come home last night I almost went out of my mind. You didn't tell me you were going to be away . . ."

Julie pushed away from her mother. "There isn't time now, Mother. I'll explain it all later. Right now we've got to do something about the rustlers. Barney McCorkle and his men are going to clean us out . . ."

"McCorkle's behind it?" exclaimed Mrs. Forest. "I never did like that man."

"He's stripped the ranch. All of the hands seem to be his people, except for—" Julie winced. "Never mind." With relief, she saw Mrs. Hubbard coming out through the door. "Mrs. Hubbard," she cried, "I've been with Jim, I just left him in Seven Oaks, but he'll be here as soon as he does some things—oh, I don't know what, but did you hear me tell Mother about the rustlers? We've got to do something immediately . . ."

"I heard," said Mrs. Hubbard. "McCorkle, your foreman, he's the man behind it?"

"Only partly; it's a long story. But they're going to steal three thousand head today because they're in a tremendous rush on account of what you did, writing to the governor and the Secretary of the Interior— Oh, bother! It's us who're going to lose most of the stock and there's nobody to stop them. Unless you help us . . ."

Mrs. Hubbard drew a deep breath, started past her mother

and Julie. "We'll get the straight of it in a minute." She saw a hand near the corral, waved to him. "Arturo! Find Briggs, tell him I want to see him here at once. And everybody else. Tell them to drop whatever they're doing and come on the run. Hurry!"

She turned back to her visitors. "We'll get this under way in quick time. Now Julie, tell it more slowly, distinctly. What has Jim found out about the rustlers?"

"They've been driving the stock into the badlands, then the outlaws have been taking over and driving it through to the Indian reservations."

"I know that," said Mrs. Hubbard crisply. "It was the only way it could have been done and I've been working on how to stop it for weeks."

"I know—we heard, Jim and I—the leader of the outlaws knows all about it and he said if the Indian agents are stopped from buying from them there wouldn't be any point in continuing with the rustling. That's why they decided to make this last big haul . . ."

Two or three ranch hands were already pounding toward the group of women in front of the ranch house. In the lead was the foreman.

"Briggs," said Mrs. Hubbard, going to meet the big man, "get every man within a reasonable distance into the saddle. I want them all well-armed, well-mounted. They're going to earn their pay today and I want you to have them assembled and ready in twenty minutes. Understand?"

"Where are we going, Mrs. Hubbard?" asked the foreman of the H-Bar-H Ranch.

"You'll get definite orders when you're ready. Move, Briggs!"

Briggs went off at a dead run. Mrs. Hubbard turned back to Julie and her mother. Mrs. Hubbard's alertness, her quick grasp of the situation and her command over the ranch hands gave Julie a slight feeling of awe. Mrs. Forest was staring at her old friend with a similar look. She had never really known Alice Hubbard.

The H-Bar-H Ranch had seen its most prosperous days after the death of Tom Hubbard eight years ago, but everyone believed that Hubbard had been the driving and directing force of the ranch, and it was assumed that he had organized the ranch so well, had laid down the principles by which it was to continue in operation, that Alice Hubbard had merely had to continue along the lines set by her husband. Mrs. Forest wondered now if Alice Hubbard had not been the force behind Tom Hubbard.

133

There was a cot against the back wall of Corbett's cell and he sat on it, elbows on his knees, hands clasped together and holding up his chin. The disaster that had overtaken him a half-hour ago had fogged his mind for awhile and he now had to think things out. He had had the situation in the palm of his hands and then Eben Smith had come before him, demanding to be killed. Except for that, Corbett would already have . . .

He groaned, shook his head.

In the cell across the aisle the other prisoner was watching Corbett. When he heard the groan he reached under his grimy pillow and produced a half-filled, half-pint bottle of whisky. He took a quick swig of the contents, then held up the bottle.

"A little snort of pain killer make you feel better?" he called across the cells. "I could slide this over to you on the floor . . ."

"No, thanks," said Corbett automatically. Then suddenly he got up and crossed to the cell door. "How'd you get that bottle in here?"

The other prisoner chuckled. "That's why I'm here. I'm the town drunk. A man likes his booze, he always knows how to get it, no matter. You got two bucks, I'll get you a bottle."

"How?" demanded Corbett.

"That's a professional secret," retorted the town drunk. "But you throw me over two dollars . . ."

"Don't fool around," snapped Corbett. "How do you do it?"

"All right, I'll tell you," said the man across the aisle. He got up and came to the door so that he was only six feet from Corbett. "I'm in here off and on. I always ask for a cell facin' the street. It don't make no difference to the sheriff, but now and then the deputy used to throw me over on your side and then it was tougher . . ."

"Get to it, man!" cried Corbett impatiently.

"I'm tellin' you—Pedro, the Mex swamper at the saloon's a friend of mine. He gets my signal . . ."

"What signal?"

The drunk took a red bandanna from his pocket. "This. I tie it to the bar in the window and when Pedro sees it he comes over and I give him the money and then when he comes back in the afternoon to clean up this place, he fetches the bottle with him. 'Course, if I got no money, it's no whisky."

"When'd you get that bottle?" asked Corbett.

"Yesterday. I been nursin' it on account it was all the

134

money I had and I've gotta stay here until tomorrow. The Judge gimme three days . . ."

"Put your signal in the window," said Corbett. "Get your man over here."

"I gotta have the two dollars."

Corbett took his money out of his pocket, separated a twenty-dollar bill and, crumpling it into a ball, threw it across the aisle. It went between a couple of bars and fell on the other prisoner's cell floor. The man scooped it up, smoothed it out and exclaimed, "A twenty!"

"That's for you," said Corbett. "Keep it until you get out, then buy yourself a real toot so you can get back in here right away." He crumpled up five more bills into balls. "And here's a hundred dollars. For Pedro."

"You crazy? For a hundred dollars you can get a barrel of whisky."

"I don't want whisky. I want a gun. Pedro can buy one for twenty dollars at Brady's store. He can keep the rest of the money . . ."

The man across the aisle stared at Corbett through the bars. "You already killed the deputy. You fixin' to take care of the sheriff?"

"I want out of here and if I've got to kill the sheriff to do it, that's too bad. But I won't kill him if I don't have to. I promise you that."

"That's a lot of money you got there," said the man across the aisle. "How much is in that wad?"

"What difference does it make? I won it playing poker. It's easy come, easy go . . ."

"I'm glad you said that because I ain't gonna be no party to any shootin'—not for no twenty dollars. I want a hundred dollars, Mister, and then I'm gonna shake the dust off this country offa me. I'm fed up with it. I want to go to Kansas City or some place a man can scrounge a meal or a drink once in awhile and where the jails are civilized. The food isn't bad here, but it's lonesome. I'm usually the only prisoner in the place and I can't sleep all the time . . ."

He stopped. Corbett was wadding up bills. He threw them across the aisle one by one. All of them went into the cell and the prisoner gathered them up.

He stowed them away in various pockets, then went to the window and knotted his bandanna about one of the bars.

The next hour was the longest one that Corbett had ever endured. He paced his cell, sat down on the cot and once or twice even tried to close his eyes and get a nap. It was no use. He was too restless to remain still.

And then, at last, the man across the aisle, who was standing up on his cot peering through his barred window, turned. "He's coming!"

"Don't let him get away," cried Corbett. *"Make* him get the gun."

"Pedro can use the money, he's got about six-seven kids and—" he raised up on his toes and began speaking in Spanish. He rattled off a string of sentences, listened, then spoke again. Finally he turned to Corbett. "He says he needs his job here. The sheriff pays him ten dollars a month to clean up the joint . . ."

"Offer him two hundred," cried Corbett. "I need that gun as soon as possible. Today—within the hour . . ."

The town drunk let go with another barrage of Spanish, then began handing out the crumpled bills. After a moment he stepped down from the cot. "He wants the other hundred when he brings the gun."

"Is he going to bring it right away—or wait for this afternoon?"

"He's going to try." The drunk came to the cell door. "Of course you know that means another hundred for me too. I ain't gonna take no less'n the Mex."

"All right, all right," snapped Corbett irritably. "Just don't carry it too far . . ."

He got the money in shape and tossed it over to the other prisoner, who then resumed his position by the window.

Fifteen minutes went by, then the man across the aisle became alert.

"He's got the gun all right." Then, "He's headed this way."

There was a strenuous wait then. Two minutes, three and finally the drunk reached to the window with the money. The bills were snatched away from him. There was a moment's wait, then the revolver was thrust through the bars.

"Gracias, amigo," exclaimed the town drunk.

He stepped down from his cot, came swiftly to the door and, crouching, reached through the bars and slid the revolver across to Corbett. It landed against the metal door with a clang that Corbett knew must have been heard out in the sheriff's office, if there was anyone in it. He scooped up the gun, stepped quickly to the cot and thrust the gun under the pillow.

Across the corridor the other prisoner said, "It's almost dinner time, but with the deputy not around I wonder if the sheriff's gonna feed us."

Chapter Twenty-Seven

Twenty-seven H-Bar-H hands, sixteen of whom were professional fighters, had left the headquarters of the Hubbard Ranch. The three women had remained behind, of course, but Julie, waiting for Corbett to come out to the ranch, could not remain in the house. She explored the buildings, visited the corrals.

An hour passed and she went in and announced to both her mother and Mrs. Hubbard that she was going to Seven Oaks. Mrs. Forest showed concern. "You won't do anything —reckless?"

"No, I just want to see what's keeping Jim." Her mother and Mrs. Hubbard exchanged quick looks at the casual use of Corbett's first name.

Julie went outside and mounted the horse she had borrowed from Cathy Brady, which was now completely rested. She sent it away from the Hubbard Ranch at a fine gallop, slowing down only when she was halfway to Seven Oaks. She put it into a swift lope again as she entered the confines of the town.

As she neared the hotel she recognized Corbett's horse tied to the hitch rail and swerved to ride toward it. Gregson, who had apparently been watching her come up from inside the lobby, came to the door.

"He ain't here," he said. He pointed. "He's taken up a room at the other hotel."

"What are you talking about?" snapped Julie. "That's . . ."

"The jailhouse," retorted Gregson. "And that's where he is now. Takin' it nice and easy . . ."

"That's absurd," cried Julie. "There's been no reason to arrest Mr. Corbett and . . ."

"Murder's usually a pretty good reason," said Gregson. "Our fine detective up and killed the deputy sheriff about an hour ago. It was as purty a piece of shootin' as I ever seen and I saw the whole thing right from the beginnin'. The deputy—" he stopped.

Julie had already whirled her horse and was rushing it

across the street. She bounced to the ground and approached the veranda where Sheriff Link Brady stood watching her arrival with a heavy scowl on his big features.

"What's this about Jim Corbett?" Julie cried. "Gregson's just told me . . ."

"It's true I had to arrest him." The sheriff shook his head. "Nothin' worse than murderin' an officer of the law . . ."

"If he killed Eben Smith," said Julie angrily, "he had reason. Your so-called deputy was nothing but an outlaw and gun fighter himself. Why you ever hired him in the first place is more than anyone around here could understand. My father remarked about that more than once . . ."

"Julie," said Brady stiffly, "I've always been a friend of your family, but I've got my job to do . . ."

"Then why aren't you doing it?" flashed Julie. "Right now Barney McCorkle and his hired gang of thieves are cleaning out our entire range and you're standing here in town talking about doing your duty."

"McCorkle's your foreman," began Brady, but Julie cut him off again.

"Not any more he isn't. He's in with the people in the bad-lands and so are some other people I could name, and the law's not doing a damn thing about it. If it weren't for Mrs. Hubbard—" Julie caught herself. She had been cautioned by Mrs. Hubbard not to reveal in town that she had sent a small army to fight the rustlers.

Julie made a quick switch. "I want to see Mr. Corbett—" She started up the short flight of stairs to get to the door of the sheriff's office, but he moved to block her.

"Can't anyone see him until the Judge charges him officially."

"That's ridiculous," cried Julie. "It's important that I see him at once." Then, "Bail, isn't that what they call it, when a prisoner's released from jail while awaiting trial?"

"There's no bail for murder."

"Sheriff," said Julie earnestly, "my father's dead and mother and I are running the ranch now. Yes, we're in trouble, but that trouble's going to be wiped out in a short while. We're not going to forget your attitude in this, and neither will other people. Mrs. Hubbard, for instance, who's richer than anyone in the valley, and whose money is helping to support this town. She's—she's on our side and if you insist, I'll ride back to her ranch and have her come in to town. She'll make the bail for her—for Corbett if the Forests aren't able to do it themselves."

"It won't do no good," persisted the sheriff. "There won't be no bail made for a murderer. I wouldn't accept it even if I could—and it's not really my business to do so. The Judge decides that."

"Judge Pelkey?" cried Julie. Her eyes darted to the right side of the building which was the courthouse and where Judge Pelkey had an office.

Link Brady saw the sudden decision come into Julie's face and he moved forward. "Hold on now . . ."

But Julie was already running toward the courthouse. Brady started after her, but Julie was ahead of him. She tore open a door, piled into a small room that was plainly furnished and occupied by an elderly man.

"Judge Pelkey," cried Julie, "Sheriff Brady's holding a prisoner in jail and refuses to let me see him or . . ."

Brady came in behind Julie. "It's the detective, Judge," he said. "She insists on talking to you about putting up bail for him. I told her that there was no bail for a man held on a murder charge."

The judge nodded automatically, but Julie interposed swiftly. "Mr. Corbett's employed by one of the biggest detective agencies in the country. The Jarvis Agency of Chicago. My father sent for him when he knew—when he suspected someone was going to kill him. Mr. Corbett's employed by my mother and if he's done anything, he's done it for *us*. *We're* responsible for his actions . . ."

The judge listened carefully to Julie and began to bob his head before Julie was even finished. "What you say may very well be important at the trial. It may mean all the difference in the world to the defense . . ."

"We're not worried about the trial, Judge Pelkey," said Julie earnestly. "It's right now, today. He's got to be let out of jail. He—he was all ready to arrest the murderer of my father."

"He knew the identity of the killer?"

"Yes. That is, almost. He told me he had the case almost solved."

"That's got nothing to do with the other," exclaimed the sheriff. "This Corbett's been nothing but trouble ever since he arrived here. And he had a special hatred for Eben Smith. You saw the condition Eben was in after Corbett pistol-whipped him. He wanted to kill him then, but Eben wouldn't make a play. He took the beating rather than draw and kill the detective. But Corbett wouldn't have it any other way. This morning he finally gunned down Smith . . ."

"For which he ought to get a reward!" cried Julie. "Everybody in this valley knows what kind of man Smith was, everybody but our fine sheriff . . ."

"Now, now, Miss," protested the judge, "you're forgetting

yourself. There's no call for you to abuse the sheriff just because he's doing the job for which the voters elected him . . ."

Julie suddenly realized that she had lost. She opened her mouth to pour out more invective, but caught herself. She made a tremendous effort to compose herself, then said quietly, "You won't release Mr. Corbett on bail?"

"I don't see how I can," said the elderly judge, "if the sheriff's adamant about it . . ."

"I am," said Brady firmly.

Julie whirled and rushed out of the judge's office. The sheriff remained behind.

On the street Julie looked toward the sheriff's office and was half tempted to storm in and talk to Jim Corbett while the sheriff was next door. But while she was still debating the subject, the sheriff came out of the judge's office and the opportunity was gone.

Julie started across the street and became aware that a man a couple of buildings away was waving to her. It was Bonner, the Wells Fargo man. She suddenly recalled the things that Corbett had told her about Bonner during the night in the outlaw hideout.

She walked quickly toward him.

"Saw you talkin' to the sheriff, then you went into the judge's office," Bonner said. "I know Jim Corbett's working for you and I thought if you were going to see him you could give him a message from me."

"What is it?" asked Julie.

Bonner dropped his voice. "Somebody using your father's name sent a telegram to the detective agency, tellin' them to cancel Corbett comin' here. The telegram was sent *after* your father was, ah, killed."

Julie inhaled sharply. "Somebody sent it in his name!"

The Wells Fargo man bobbed his head. "That's what Corbett figured. I mean, that's what I told him. On account of I never took the telegram here. We figured it was sent from some other office and Corbett wanted me to find out from where. I just got the answer ten minutes ago. It was sent at Roswell."

"Who sent it?"

"That's the part that's gonna shock Mr. Corbett. It wasn't a man who sent it at all. It was a—a woman. A young woman who gave the name of—well, *your* name. Julia Forest."

"That's ridiculous," cried Julie. "I never sent such a telegram."

"I didn't say you did. I'm just telling you what the Roswell

140

agent told me on the wire. The lady told the agent her pa didn't want no one from here to know he was sending the telegram and that he sent you to Roswell."

"That's a complete lie. Whoever sent that telegram bribed the agent to tell you that I sent it."

"I don't think you could do that with Ferguson," said the Wells Fargo man, defending his fellow Wells Fargo agent.

"I suppose he's above being bribed like *all* Wells Fargo agents." There was withering contempt in Julie's tone, but when she saw the blood rush to Bonner's face she realized what she had said to the agent. "I'm sorry, Mr. Bonner," she apologized immediately. "I'm just so worked up I don't know what I'm doing or saying."

"That's all right, Miss Julie," said Bonner. "I just thought if you got a chance to talk to Mr. Corbett you'd tell him what I found out for him." He hesitated. "I was in the saloon the other night when Eben Smith exposed Corbett and I didn't blame Corbett at all for what he did to Smith later, pistol-whipping him."

"You saw the fight this morning?" asked Julie eagerly.

"Not quite. I was inside when the shooting started. I just saw the tail end of it when Corbett was down on the street, shooting at Smith. I still say Smith had it coming to him."

Julie nodded. "Thank you, Mr. Bonner. I—I'll tell Mr. Corbett what you said when I see him. If they let me see him."

She was about to start off when the agent said, "Oh—you wouldn't be going by Mrs. Hubbard's on your way home, would you? I've got a telegram here for her that I haven't been able to take out." He cleared his throat. "I've got a man here from the main office going over things. I thought maybe Mrs. Hubbard would want to see this telegram . . ."

He took it out of his pocket, crumpled, much handled.

Julie glanced at the telegram, reacted, then read it swiftly. "But this is the answer to all of our problems," she exclaimed.

The agent said, "I thought it might be important, that's why I asked if you'd take it out to Mrs. Hubbard."

"Mr. Bonner," declared Julie, her spirits suddenly soaring, "this is the best news that any of us could have heard. If it had come while my father was still alive—" she stopped, her eyes going in the direction of the sheriff's office. "Wait until this news gets around. You haven't told anyone about this, have you?"

"No, of course not. Nobody except Mr. Corbett . . ."

"Then he knows. I'm going right out and tell Mrs. Hubbard—and my mother." She started to turn away, then wheeled back and started forward, headed for the Brady store.

She burst into the store, passed Jeff Brady with a cool nod, and went to the rear of the store where Cathy was behind the post office wicket.

"Cathy," she exclaimed softly, "I've got some news for you, something that ought to make you very happy."

Cathy looked at her curiously. "What?"

Julie thrust the telegram she had just received under the wicket so that Cathy could read it. "You know what that means?" she asked enthusiastically. "All the rustling will stop —at once. If there's no market for stolen beef nobody will bother to steal any. That means you can marry Tracy safely now, knowing that nobody's going to steal his cattle . . ."

Cathy's eyes were still on the telegram. She was apparently studying it, trying to translate its brief message into terms that she could understand. She looked up at Julie.

"I don't understand. This is addressed to Alice Hubbard . . ."

"I've just come from there," replied Julie. "We've become very close friends in the last few days. My mother's out there right now. The Wells Fargo man gave me this to deliver and I'm going out there now. What should be done is to make a great big poster of this telegram and put it up here where everybody in town will see it!"

Cathy's tongue came out, moistened her lips. "Yes, that would be fine, wouldn't it?" She glanced at the telegram again. "I didn't know Mrs. Hubbard was this kind of a woman. I mean, sending telegrams to the Secretary of the Interior, to the governor. If it'd been your father, yes, but— she's only a woman . . ."

"She's a very wonderful woman," said Julie. "But I mustn't tell you everything. I've got a secret myself, but I can't tell you about it now. Later—maybe by the time you and Tracy get married. Yes, I'll tell you then—for your wedding present." She flashed a beautiful smile at Cathy as she took the telegram from under the wicket and started for the door.

This time she did not even bother to nod to Cathy's father. She went out of the store and did not hear Jeff Brady's roar of rage, or the thing he said about Julie—without using her name.

Chapter Twenty-Eight

It was the custom to feed whatever prisoners there were in the jail between twelve and one o'clock. The food, ordered earlier in the morning, was brought over from the hotel dining room, and it was the habit of the deputy sheriff to take it back to the cells.

The town drunk told this to Corbett and the latter was patiently waiting in his cell for the sheriff, or whoever, to bring the noonday meal. He would then make his play. He looked at his watch at eleven-thirty, again at twenty minutes to twelve. It was then, when Julie had gone off to his brother's store, that Link Brady decided to go into his office and into the cell block.

He came heavily along the cells, stopped before Corbett's. "Thought you'd be interested, Corbett," he said, his lips curling in a sneer. "That sweetie of yours . . ."

"Who?" exclaimed Corbett.

"The Forest offspring, who else? She's just made a big scene with Judge Pelkey, trying to get you out on bail." The sheriff sneered openly. "She didn't succeed."

Corbett sat erect on the edge of the cot.

Brady continued, "You know why the judge didn't let you out on bail?"

"You," said Corbett. "You resisted it."

"I didn't resist," snapped the sheriff. "I came right out and told the judge I wouldn't let you out. You're not stepping out of this jail until you go to court. *If* you go to court. I thought you'd be interested. Thought I'd tell you so you know where you stand."

"Thanks, Sheriff," said Corbett bitterly. "And now I'll tell you where *you* stand. The Secretary of the Interior—yes, in Washington, D.C.—issued an order yesterday to all the Indian agents in this state to stop buying beef."

The sheriff's big features seemed to collapse for one moment, but then he made an effort and his face became one big scowl again.

"What's that got to do with me?" he snarled.

"Nothing, maybe," said Corbett. "Except . . ."

His left hand, that was lying on the cot, the fingertips just an inch from the pillow, went under the pillow, came out with the revolver in his hand. The sheriff saw the gun, started back and his hand went down to his own gun.

Corbett threw the gun from his left hand to his right, cocked the hammer and said softly, "Go ahead, Sheriff, reach! If you're faster than Eben Smith, you might even live . . ."

A shudder ran through the sheriff's entire body, then he became as stiff as a hard oak tree.

Corbett gestured with the gun. "Bring out your key, Sheriff. Nice and easy . . ."

Brady gasped, then grabbed for the final straw. "I haven't got it. It's—it's in the office."

"That's too bad," said Corbett, "because I'm going to count to three and if the key isn't in this lock by that time you're a dead man. One, two . . ."

"No!" howled the sheriff. He lunged forward, fumbling in his vest pocket. His trembling fingers brought out the key, almost dropped it in his haste. He poked at the keyhole twice, got the key in the hole, then turned it.

Corbett pulled the cell door inward. He stepped to one side, gestured for the sheriff to enter the cell. Apprehensively, the sheriff took a tentative step forward.

"You're not going to . . . ?"

"No," said Corbett, "I'm not." Then as the sheriff stepped past him, his right hand went up, came down in a savage smash. The revolver barrel crunched through the sheriff's hat, thudded into his head.

Brady fell forward. His head and chest struck the cot, but the force of his driven fall ricocheted him off the cot to the floor. He lay still in a crumpled heap.

Corbett looked down at him a moment, then holstered his expensively-purchased revolver and, stooping, caught the sheriff under both armpits. He raised him up, dumped him on the cot, then straightened him out so that the unconscious Brady lay on his back.

He went to the door, took out the key and stepped out into the aisle. He extended the key to his fellow jail inmate, but the town drunk promptly shook his head.

"Nope, not me, they're turning me loose tomorrow and I don't want no part of *that*."

Corbett put the key in the other prisoner's door lock, turned it. "I've got some things to do and I don't want him to crowd me too closely. He'll be out for ten, fifteen minutes. Do me a favor—because I haven't got the time. Tie his hands and feet, put a gag in his mouth. Then lock your door and throw the key through the window. That'll hold him for a spell and he won't be able to pin it on you. All right?"

He pushed open the drunk's cell door.

The man came forward, shaking his head. "Man and boy, I've seen some rough ones, but you're the best of 'em." Admiration was in his voice. "A real curly wolf!"

Corbett left the cell block, going to the sheriff's office. He stepped out, walked swiftly across the veranda and down to the street. He turned right and crossed the sidewalk in an oblique route, missing both the Wells Fargo office and the saloon. He reached the far sidewalk in front of Brady's store.

He entered.

Cathy Brady was in the store alone. She reacted visibly when she saw Corbett. "You want my father, Mr. Corbett? He—he isn't here just now."

"I know. I just saw him ride off. It's you I want to talk to, Cathy."

"Me? I, uh, you want some stamps? I know there isn't any mail for you."

Corbett nodded easily. "I just wanted to ask you a couple of questions, Cathy. Nothing important really." He could see that she was highly nervous and his calmness was not doing anything to alleviate it. "This morning, Cathy, when we met you at Tracy Holderman's you hadn't really spent the night there, had you?"

A flush swept over her face. "You're not going to keep bringing *that* up, are you, Mister—Mister Corbett?"

"It's Mister now, Cathy? I'm afraid I *have* to bring it up."

"I told you I was there all night," Cathy said fiercely. "We're engaged, we're going to be married in less than a week and I don't care what you or anybody else thinks about it. Do you want it plainer than that? I spent the night with Tracy. We—we slept together."

"You're willing to let the world know you're that kind of a woman?" asked Corbett, a trace of mockery coming into his voice. "Well, maybe you are. You're also a liar, Cathy."

"Don't talk to me like that," she said in a half-whisper.

"Why not, Cathy? A liar isn't as bad as a—a person who reads other people's mail."

"I don't," she protested. "I—I just look at the postcards once in awhile."

"The other day when I mailed a letter," Corbett went on, "you told me that it would go out on the evening stage. I didn't stop to think then that if there's an eastbound stagecoach, there's also one going west—one that comes here from the east. A morning stage that arrives here very early. Around six, is it?"

145

"What's that go to do with—" began Cathy, then stopped.

"I believed what I saw this morning," Corbett said. "And what you told me—confessed, rather. You'd spent the night with Tracy. Actually, you didn't. You were here in town all night. But you got the morning mail and you found a letter in it that you decided to take right out to Tracy. You got there very early, seven, seven-thirty. And you were leaving to get back to town when we got to Tracy's."

"That's not true," exclaimed Cathy. "It's a lie!"

"Is it, Cathy?"

"All right, what of it? Tracy was expecting a letter. A very important letter. He'd told me about it and when I saw it in the mail, I rode out to his place."

"In other words, you just delivered his mail to him?"

"There's no law against that!"

"No," said Corbett, "not if the letter was addressed to him. But was it? Or was it someone else's letter you took out there? Was it a letter addressed to—Mrs. Alice Hubbard?"

Cathy almost screamed the reply. "No!"

"Mrs. Hubbard hasn't been to town today," said Corbett. "So there ought to be a letter for her in her box."

"There isn't!"

"Mind if I take a look?"

He started for the post office section. Cathy scurried along behind the counter to block him, but he reached the section, took her arm and moved her aside. He began studying the names pasted on the box slots.

Cathy cried out, "It's against the law to interfere with the United States mail . . ."

"That's right, Cathy," said Corbett. "It's a Federal offense. Let's see, yes, H—Hubbard." He reached to the slot, took down a large official-looking envelope. He read the printed return office address: The Governor's Office. He turned the envelope over and ran a fingertip along the sealed envelope flap.

"You're very good at it, Cathy," he said. "I guess you've had a lot of practice. You can hardly tell this has been steamed open and pasted down again."

"Put it back," said Cathy. "Put it back or I—I'll report you."

"Who'll you report me to? Your uncle, the sheriff? His isn't a Federal office." He thrust the envelope into his pocket. "I may be going out to the Hubbard Ranch. I'll deliver it personally to Mrs. Hubbard. Sort of special delivery . . ."

His attitude suddenly changed, became brisk as hardness came into his voice. "It *had* to be you. Every clue I picked up along the way somehow had something to do with the

146

mail. Why, even up in the hills Salinger, the head man of the outlaws—he knew that Mrs. Hubbard had corresponded with the governor about investigating the Indian agents, who were buying stolen beef." He produced the envelope again. "I haven't read this letter, but I can make an awfully good guess as to what's in it. The governor's had word from the Secretary of the Interior that he's going to end the cattle rustling in Seven Oaks Valley—by issuing an order to the Indian agents to stop buying beef, pending an inquiry and investigation of the agents. You had to get that to Tracy Holderman in a hurry, didn't you?"

"Are you accusing Tracy Holderman of—of being a rustler?" cried Cathy.

"What's worse?" asked Corbett. "A rustler, or a—murderer?"

The back of her hand flew to Cathy's mouth. Corbett went on remorselessly, "Why was Sam Forest murdered, Cathy? Shall I tell you? Because he'd written a letter to Chicago hiring a detective. Isn't that why? *But who knew that, Cathy?* Sam Forest didn't even tell his wife or Julie. *You* knew it, though, because you'd steamed open his letter—and told Tracy Holderman . . ."

"No, no!" wailed Cathy.

"You didn't pull the trigger, Cathy," said Corbett, "but you might just as well have, because you're as guilty of Forest's murder as—Tracy Holderman."

He turned abruptly away from her, walked out from behind the post office department and out of the store.

On the street Corbett walked heavily along the sidewalk, oblivious of the stares of the townspeople who had seen him taken to jail that morning.

Gregson was in the doorway of the hotel, but he did not accost Corbett. Corbett went to his horse, untied it from the hitch rail and mounted. He rode west out of Seven Oaks.

147

Chapter Twenty-Nine

Jeff Brady found his prospective son-in-law seated on the sawbuck behind the house. Tracy must have heard him ride up, but he did not leave his perch to come forward. Tracy Holderman was trying to come to an important decision and it was not easy.

Brady dismounted and looked down at Tracy.

"Well, Tracy?" he said.

The younger man looked up. "Everything's blown to hell, hasn't it?"

"There may be some pieces to pick up," suggested Brady, "but we've got to decide one way or the other what we're going to do."

"I don't see that there's anything to do but light out," said Tracy.

Brady scowled. "That's easy for you, Tracy, you've got twenty-five thousand stashed away. You can pick it up and run. What you've got here, hell," he showed his contempt. "It isn't worth a pot of beans!"

"I worked eight years for this," snapped Tracy.

"Yes, yes, I've heard that often enough. But what did you start with? Nothing. I've got a lot of money invested in my business. I can't just run away." He drew a deep breath. "Link's got the detective in jail. He don't have to talk."

Tracy looked at his prospective father-in-law curiously. "What do you mean?"

"Judge Pelkey says there's no bail for murder."

"You still have to let him talk to a lawyer," said Tracy. "And what about the Forests and," scowling, "that damn Hubbard woman? She's the one spoiled the whole thing. Writing to the governor, the Secretary of the Interior . . ."

He stopped as the pounding of galloping horses was suddenly heard. He stepped away from Brady to look down the trail that led to the main road. He let out a groan.

Brady stepped over beside Tracy. "Your brothers and the old man!"

"Damn," swore Tracy, "damn it to hell!"

"Stand up to them," snapped Brady.

Tracy swallowed hard and watched the members of his family approach.

Pete Junior was in the lead. His horse was still moving when he leaped to the ground and came striding forward. He came swiftly toward Tracy and without a word swung his fist at Tracy. The blow caught Tracy high on the cheekbone and drove him back.

"You little squirt," snarled Pete Junior, "what the hell do you think you're doing?"

Tracy held his hand against his bruised cheek, but made no reply. Quincy dismounted, but stood aside until the old man had climbed down from his horse.

"Now, now, boys," he said soothingly. "You promised me you'd behave." He smiled unctuously. "We just wanna have a little talk with Tracy, that's all." He suddenly nodded to Jeff Brady. "Howdy, Brady, still cheating customers at the store?"

"You don't like my prices, take your business elsewhere," retorted Jeff Brady. "I told you that long ago."

"Sure, sure, no hard feelings?" Old Pete turned back to Tracy. "Your ma died when you was on'y a tadpole and you never had the benefit of her raisin' but I tried to take over for her and if I told you once, I told you a thousand times, honesty's the best policy." He pointed a forefinger at his youngest son. "You forget that, boy?"

Tracy suddenly flared up. "Save your preaching for Quincy and Pete, you sanctimonious old hypocrite. I've had enough of it."

Old Pete Holderman drew back in mock chagrin. "Is that a way to talk to your old pa?" He turned to Quincy and young Pete. "What do you think of your brother, boys?"

Quincy said, "He needs a good lickin'."

"Say the word, Pa, and I'll beat the hell out of him," said Pete Junior.

Old Pete shook his head. "It ain't right for brothers to be fightin' each other." He stepped forward suddenly and gave Tracy a crack in the face with his open palm. The blow landed on Tracy's right cheek, already bruised by his oldest brother's fist. Then the old man rocked Tracy again, but on the left cheek.

"I told you, Tracy, over and over," he said. "You don't steal from your own family. Brandin' a maverick once in awhile or cuttin' out a beef for the table, there's nothin' wrong with that, but stealing from your own family, Tracy, there's nothin' lower than that."

"I never touched your cattle," cried Tracy. "Maybe one or two of them got mixed in sometime, when we were in a hurry, but I told McCorkle to stay off your ranch."

"You didn't tell him hard enough," said Old Pete. "We caught him an hour ago with six hundred head of Lightning brand beef." He chuckled in satisfaction. "That's one rustler won't be doin' no more rustlin'."

"You killed McCorkle?" cried Jeff Brady.

"Who, me?" asked Pete Holderman innocently. "You know I don't hold with killings and such. We may have roughed him up a little, but it was his own boys who done him in—when they heard that there wasn't no more market for prime beef."

Jeff Brady drew a deep breath. "Pete, I've known you for a long time. I knew you when you first came down from the hills and I've watched that herd of yours grow. It's practically a miracle and—"

"Now, now, Jeff," chided Old Pete.

"Listen to me through," went on Brady. "There's a detective in town . . ."

"He's still around?" cried old Pete. "I thought we discouraged him a leetle bit."

"You should have finished him," snapped Brady. "My brother's got him in jail now, but if he talks to the right people, or if he appears in court, it's going to be pretty hard on some of the people around here." He nodded toward Tracy. "Especially your son. *Corbett mustn't be allowed to talk.*"

Old Pete cocked his head to one side. "Don't hint, Brady. Come out with it, lay it on the line."

"Kill him," said Brady savagely. "Kill the detective and Tracy'll pull through."

"And you too?" scowled Old Pete.

"Nobody can prove anything on me," said Brady.

"The hell they can't. You're in it as deep as Tracy."

Jeff Brady shook his head. "Tracy organized it. He made the deal with the boys in the hills. He was in charge of the operations down here."

"Who killed Sam Forest?" cried Old Pete.

Jeff Brady couldn't resist a furtive glance at Tracy. "I don't know," he said, "that's not important."

"The hell it ain't," snarled Old Pete. "That was murder. Rustlin's one thing, but murder's another. That's one thing I ain't gonna do, not at my age."

"Not even to protect Tracy?" snapped Brady.

Old Pete turned to his son again. He looked at him moodily. Then suddenly he struck Tracy again. He rocked his head to the left, straightened it with another blow. Tracy covered his face with his arms, tried to back away. Old Pete followed him.

"You chicken-livered sneak," Old Pete snarled. "You

couldn't even go up to him like a man. You had to shoot him in the back with a shotgun." He delivered one final blow, then turned away. "You're no son of mine. I wash my hands of you." He gestured to his older sons. "Come on, boys, we'll go home."

"You gonna just leave him like this?" asked young Pete.

"If he's man enough to kill the detective, we'll still keep our mouths shut. If he isn't, he's played the tune, let him dance—alone."

Old Pete went to his horse and climbed up on it. His sons followed him. Jeff Brady and his prospective son-in-law watched the three men ride off. Then Brady turned to Tracy.

"Well, Tracy?"

Tracy Holderman drew a deep breath, let it out with a whoosh. Then without a word he walked toward the log cabin. He went inside and came out almost immediately. He was carrying a double-barreled shotgun.

Chapter Thirty

Mrs. Forest was inside the Hubbard house, but Julie was outside with Alice Hubbard when they saw a trio of horsemen come swiftly from the west.

"It's Briggs," said Mrs. Hubbard.

"Your foreman!" cried Julie. Then dismay came over her. "They're all that's left . . ."

Mrs. Hubbard shook her head. "No, I know Briggs. He hasn't been in any fight."

She began to walk forward. Briggs came up at a swift trot, dismounted near his employer. He said instantly, "There wasn't any trouble, ma'am. It was over before we got there."

"Thank God," said Alice Hubbard fervently.

"I left the boys out there, just in case," went on Briggs. "We caught a couple of the—the rustlers. They said they'd just got word that they were wasting their time. The government's stepped in and closed the Indian agencies who've been buying the beef."

"Yes," said Mrs. Hubbard, "that's true. I received a telegram from the Secretary of the Interior to that effect." She indicated Julie. "Julie Forest brought it out."

A light frown came over Briggs' face. "There was a dead man. I was told that Pete Holderman and his boys killed him. It was—" Briggs looked at Julie—"your foreman, Barney McCorkle."

A gasp was torn from Julie, but she recovered quickly and turned to Mrs. Hubbard. "I'm going back to town. Please—come with me. We can get Jim out of jail now, I'm sure."

"It won't be necessary," said Mrs. Hubbard. Her eyes were looking beyond Julie.

Julie whirled. "It's Jim!"

Corbett was riding easily toward the ranch yard. Julie ran forward a few feet, then stopped. Corbett dismounted.

"He let you go?" cried Julie.

Corbett did not reply. He came toward Alice Hubbard. He took a letter from his pocket. "I picked up your mail, ma'am. The envelope's been steamed open, but it wasn't me that did it."

Alice Hubbard barely glanced at the letter. She nodded to Briggs. "Briggs, this is my son, Jim Corbett."

Briggs, already reaching forward to shake hands with Corbett, exclaimed softly. He recovered quickly.

"Howdy, Corbett," he said simply.

Corbett nodded acknowledgment. He turned back to Alice Hubbard.

Julie said quickly, "The rustling's been stopped, Jim. Briggs just told us. There—there wasn't any fight at all. But Barney —he's dead!"

"And Tracy?" asked Corbett.

"Tracy Holderman?" exclaimed Briggs. "He's been involved in this?"

"The *good* Holderman," said Corbett. "He was the leader." He turned toward his horse. "I guess I've got to go and pick him up."

"Why you?" cried Julie. "Haven't you done enough? The sheriff—"

"The sheriff?" repeated Corbett. "He's Jeff Brady's brother and Jeff Brady's in it too. Along with his daughter Cathy. It was she who steamed open the mail and told Tracy." He looked at Alice Hubbard. "She knew that you'd written to the governor. She read all of the letters and passed the information on to Tracy." He paused. "She read the letter that Sam Forest wrote to my agency . . ."

"Oh, no!" wailed Julie. "Not—Cathy!"

"They knew I was a detective when I first came here."

"The Wells Fargo man," said Julie, remembering. "He—he told me to tell you. The telegram to the agency that was sent after my father was killed—he said it was sent from Roswell by a—a girl who gave my name . . ."

"Cathy," said Corbett.

Tracy Holderman, accompanied by Jeff Brady, entered the sheriff's office and heard Link Brady yelling from inside the cell block. They went in and found the sheriff raging. He had loosened the gag about his mouth, but he was still tied hand and foot.

"There's a key in the desk," howled the sheriff. "Get it and let me out of this."

It was his brother who went to find the key. Tracy stayed by the cell that had lately been occupied by Jim Corbett. "He's escaped?" he asked.

The sheriff let go with a stream of invectives.

Jeff Brady was still going through the desk drawer when the front door of the sheriff's office was pushed open and Cathy came in. She had been standing in front of the store

153

when Brady and Tracy had dismounted before the court-house.

"Dad," she cried, "I've got to talk to you—and Tracy."

"I know," said Jeff Brady. "The detective's escaped."

"That's what it's about," said Cathy. "He—he knows everything!"

Jeff Brady found the key. He looked at his daughter and heaved a sigh. "He's got to be stopped, Cathy. Everything'll be all right if—if we find Corbett."

Tracy Holderman came out of the cell block. He was followed by a scream from the imprisoned sheriff. Jeff Brady shook his head, went past Tracy into the cell block.

Tracy Holderman and Cathy looked at one another. "You know, Cathy?" asked Tracy.

She nodded. "It isn't too late, Tracy. Not—not if Corbett can be stopped."

"I know," said Tracy Holderman.

Cathy's eyes widened. Then her glance fell to the shotgun in Tracy Holderman's hands.

Jim Corbett was harnessing the Forest team of horses to the buckboard when the three men rode in from the road toward the ranch yard of the Hubbard Ranch. The women were all in the house but, as Tracy and the two Bradys rode up, Julie came running out. She saw the new arrivals and started swiftly toward Corbett.

"Go back," he called to her, "go into the house."

She stopped. "You can't fight them alone, Jim," she cried.

Link Brady heard her. "There isn't going to be any fight. This man's broken out of jail and I'm going to take him back, that's all."

Alice Hubbard came out of the house. "You're not taking anyone from my property," she said. "You've been a disgrace as a sheriff and I'm going to make it my business to see that you're removed from office." She gestured suddenly to someone beyond the group. "Briggs, bring some of the boys!"

"No, ma'am," Corbett said quickly. "This is my fight and I'll handle it myself."

"Jim," said Alice Hubbard poignantly, "not now—not after all these years!"

He shook his head. "I've got to, ma'am. Go back into the house. Julie, you too . . ."

Briggs and a half-dozen men were coming forward. Corbett gestured to them. "Stay out of this!" He faced Link Brady squarely. "I'm not surrendering, Brady."

Link Brady looked nervously toward the H-Bar-H hands. He said, "If there's any shooting here, you'll be responsible

154

for it, Corbett." He whipped suddenly to Tracy Holderman, who was standing a few feet to one side, gripping the double-barreled shotgun. "Or you, Tracy." He sneered. "The *good* Holderman!"

Tracy Holderman licked his dry lips with his tongue. "I've had enough of that *good* stuff. I've had enough of it to last me the rest of my life."

"That won't be for long," taunted the sheriff. "You're going to stand a murder charge that I don't think you can beat."

Tracy Holderman said, "I tried to get away from it. I broke with my family and I worked. I did eight years of back-breaking work. I worked from early morning to late at night and it wasn't any good. I couldn't even get married because I was too poor. Everybody around me was getting rich except me." The bitterness in his voice suddenly changed to mimicry. "Get yourself a job, Tracy, give it up." He shot an angry look around toward Jeff Brady. "You're as much to blame as anyone. You sent Salinger out to me, after telling me that you wouldn't let Cathy marry a pauper."

"You always were a weakling," retorted Jeff Brady. "Cathy had more spunk in her little finger than you had in your whole body. Your father proved that this morning, Tracy. You stood there and let him slap you in front of me. I never saw a more sickening thing in my life—" He stopped, suddenly aghast as Tracy Holderman spun around, the shotgun pointing at his prospective father-in-law.

"Damn you," said Tracy. "Damn you and Cathy both . . ."

Jeff Brady clawed at his pocket, but it was too late. The shotgun thundered and Jeff Brady was knocked back a good three feet before his body crumpled to the ground.

It was a double-barreled shotgun and there was another lethal blast in it. Tracy swung the gun around toward Corbett, but Corbett had no intention of letting himself be cut in half. His revolver was already in his hand. It cracked sharply and his bullet went into the helpless Tracy Holderman with a thud. Tracy stumbled. He fell forward to his knees, but he was still trying to hold up the shotgun.

His dying finger pulled the trigger. The gun muzzle was away from Corbett by then, but the charge caught the sheriff in the legs just as he was drawing his own gun. His scream was heard inside the house, to which Alice Hubbard and Julie had already retreated.

Later, much later, after Julie and her mother had left the H-Bar-H Ranch in their buckboard, Corbett went to his horse.

As he was about to mount, Alice Hubbard strode up to him.

"Where are you going?"

"Seven Oaks," he replied. "I've got to make my report and, well, I guess I've got to be on my way."

"Where, Jim? Where is this place you've got to be going to?"

"Chicago, ma'am."

"Quit," she said, "write Jarvis a letter and tell him you've quit."

"Why?" he asked. "Why would I do that?"

"Because I'm tired, Jim, I'm tired of trying to be a man and run this place. I need a man here, Jim. I've needed one for a long, long time . . ."

He looked at her soberly for a long time.

Alice Hubbard said evenly, "I talked it over with Julie before she left for home. She wants you to stay. She—she asked me to tell you."

Corbett said evenly, "Maybe—maybe it'll work out."